The P

To
your gift

tain and ~~about themselves~~ and ~~the world~~ around them. In fact, at every stage of development, toys are important tools of play that help children learn. Just as a chef needs all sorts of ingredients to make a tasty dish, children need a rich mix of playthings to develop their imagination, thinking skills, and physical growth.

We can help you find your way through Toyland. Each year we put hundreds of the newest playthings to the test to find the ones with real play power.

The result: a book that gives you important information about choosing toys—**Oppenheim Toy Portfolio 1999 Edition: The Best Toys For Kids,** the sixth annual guide that you'll use all through the coming year. And to help you even further, we have teamed up with Energizer to offer a toll-free toyline—1 (800) KIDS-450 (English) and 1 (800) 448-7084 (Spanish)—which highlights the best and brightest gifts for the holidays.

SO, relax....we're taking the guesswork out of toys so you can enjoy the holidays!

Battery Basics

Proper battery care will help keep the fun going and going. Just remember:

- Make sure you're always powered up for play! With the new Energizer® Advanced Formula batteries, you'll get unsurpassed play time out of today's most demanding devices.

- When changing batteries, never mix old and new batteries.

- Never remove the battery from your smoke detector to power a toy.

- Do not store batteries loose in a drawer. They can short each other out.

- Check toy packaging carefully to see if batteries are included. Nothing is more disappointing than a new toy and no batteries.

- Store batteries at room temperature.

OFFICIAL MAIL-IN CERTIFICATE	**EXPIRATION DATE: 3/31/99**

To receive your Free Energizer Bunny® Bean Bag Toy, complete and mail this certificate with: One (1) proof-of-purchase symbol from one **Energizer**® Battery Family Pack (AAA-12, AA-12, C-8, D-8, 9V-4) and your Target cash register receipt with amount of purchase price circled.

Limit one (1) Energizer Bunny® per individual or address. No certificates submitted by groups or organizations will be honored. Offer good for residents of U.S.A. only. Allow eight (8) weeks for shipment. OFFICIAL CERTIFICATES REQUIRED; REPRODUCTIONS ARE VOID. Void where prohibited, licensed, taxed or restricted by law. Offer rights not transferable. Requests received after offer ends void. **OFFER ENDS 3/31/99**. Cash value 1/20¢.

MAIL TO:
TARGET ENERGIZER® PROGRAM
P.O. Box 460605
St. Louis, MO 63146-7605

Name _____

Address _____

City _____ State _____ Zip _____
                                        (required)

OPPENHEIM TOY PORTFOLIO

1999 Edition

The Best Toys For Kids

Joanne Oppenheim
and **Stephanie Oppenheim**
with **James Oppenheim,** *Technology Editor*

Illustrations by **Joan Auclair**

With thanks to our family and the many other families who helped us test for the best.
—Joanne, Stephanie, & James

Designed by Joan Auclair

ISBN: 0-9664823-1-X

Contents

Introduction

Dear Readers:

In this sixth annual edition you'll find the results of another year's search for quality products. With so many choices offered, it's harder than ever to know what products have real value. Few parents have the budget or time to sift through the duds and turn up those memorable products that will entertain, engage, and fit their child's developing needs. That's what we do for you.

To make shopping quick and easy, you will find our lists of this year's award-winning and top-rated products in the opening pages of this book. In addition to our Platinum Award Winners list, you'll find lists of outstanding products for group play, parent-child interactions, and office quiet time, as well as top-rated multicultural, and gender-free products.

You'll find full descriptions of these as well as other excellent new products along with shopping information in the age-appropriate chapters of the book. As always, we've included Blue Chip classics, since we believe it would be a shame for kids to miss such products just because they weren't invented yesterday.

While it's hard to believe, last year's edition is already out-of-date. Over 60% of this year's guide is entirely new—responding to the thousands of new choices introduced this year, as well as products that are no longer available.

While we tested plenty of products that just didn't work or live up to our expectations, in the end we were delighted with the range of wonderful choices available to consumers this year.

What are the trends for '99?
- **Great choices for infants & toddlers.** Last year we saw a dramatic increase in the number of innovative toys for babies. This year, the trend continues, coupled with many exciting choices for toddlers that match their new-

found mobility. We welcome these products that reflect the growing awareness of the value of children's play from the start.

- **Creativity and imagination.** There are more quality products to spark creative and imaginative play—toys that foster language and storytelling, the underpinnings for reading and writing. Building with blocks, painting at the easel, or acting out stories in costumes or with puppets—all provide the kinds of play that allow children to express their feelings and explore their own creative power. It's through such play that the storytellers, scientists, artists, and inventors of tomorrow grow.

- **Positive role models.** Barbie has joined the WNBA and comes with her own hoop dreams. Barbie's pal Ken is more than a dancing fool or a dude who surfs. In 1999 Ken is a pediatrician.

- **Remote control toys for all ages.** From music in the nursery to pets toddlers can control or vehicles that multiple kids can play with together, there are new uses for remote controls this year.

- **Technology in Toyland.** This year it seems like everyone has an interactive doll to challenge Actimates Barney. (As you may remember, Barney interacts with your child, VCR, and computer). We are also seeing new and exciting robotic toys from Lego Mindstorms that will be programmed with your computer. Like any new use of technology, all are not equally good. We will continue to watch this market and report on our website.

- **A return to basics.** Yo-yos are back for a new generation. In fact, many of the toys we played with as kids are having major birthdays—Hot Wheels and Lite Brite are both over 30 and Scrabble is 50! Many of yesterday's toys are what we call "Blue Chip Classics." We'll help remind you when it's age appropriate to bring home some of your old favorites.

- **Collecting trends.** Marking a kinder and gentler toyland, kids continue to collect Beanie babies instead of action figures with violent agendas. This year almost every company had its own version of a bean bag toy. And if you don't want to buy them there are several kits so kids can make them.

- **Gender bending.** We were delighted to find less gender color-coding in toy kitchens, dishes, trikes, and costumes. Since these are products enjoyed by both boys and girls, it's refreshing to find more and more gender-free choices. Craft kits continue to be less gender-specific—sure, there are gobs of jewelry kits, but many other kits with history and science themes are interesting to both girls and boys.

- **More for your money.** When we looked at our winners, we realized that there are many quality choices for under $20.

On the down side...

- **French fries** are big this year—plastic fries, that is. We've seen dolls that eat them, toy kitchens that cook them, and toy stores that sell them. Too bad that pretend play props are reinforcing a fried food habit that we all need less of—not more.

- Following on the success of Ernie and Elmo, there's a whole lot of **snoring and giggling** going on this year—they seem to be the sound chips of choice.

- **Virtual toys.** While virtual pets seem to have cooled off in popularity, this year we saw programmable teddy bears, dolls, and cars. Unfortunately, the original virtual pets have been gender-coded with pink themes for girls and more aggressive themes for boys.

- Get your tool chest ready! We continue to see products that require **more assembly** by the consumer. Manufacturers claim that toy retailers want smaller boxes. Bottom line remains: leave plenty of time to pre-assemble! If you're not particularly handy, you may want to pay a little extra to have the store do the work for you. No toy (excluding construction toys) should take hours to put together.

- **Age labels continue to be extremely misleading.** There's nothing wrong with your child. This is what you need to know: toys marked "not for children under 3," are crucial for safety because of small parts and we urge you to follow this guideline, but that is just one aspect of what makes a product age-appropriate. We continue to find toys marked for babies that are more appropriate for two year olds; many of the novelty dolls we tested (and liked) are marked for 18 mos. & up, but we found no child under the age of 3 who could make them work. We found building sets and craft kits that are mismarked and required intensive parent involvement.

- **Dangerous packaging.** We are alarmed by the number of toys that are being packaged in large and mid-sized plastic bags. We find the warning on these packages inadequate, given the safety hazard they pose to young children. We urge you to throw the bags away immediately.

- **Noisy toys.** There are a greater number of very loud toys (even for infants). We were amazed to learn that by law, toys can be louder than a power drill! With the help of The League for the Hard of Hearing, a nonprofit group that has brought attention to the issue of toys and hearing loss, we continue to monitor this issue. We have included more information in our Safety Guidelines section.

- What's in a name? **Make no assumptions.** As always, we find that a company can make both gems and duds in the same year. A brand name does not guarantee that a toy will work, or that the rules will make sense, or that all the pieces will be in the construction set.

We're often asked why we don't write about all the products that don't work. The fact is that there isn't room. We do tend to write more negative reviews in our newsletter and on our website. In this book we want to share the good news and there is also plenty of that this year. We'd like to thank all of the families that contribute to this book.

As always, we welcome your feedback on the selections. **You can write, or visit our Website: www.toyportfolio.com.** For new readers, you'll find our review process and criteria for our award program below.

Happy playing!

How We Select the Best

We shop for children year-round—only we get to do what most parents wish they could do before they buy. We open the toys, run the videos, read the books, play the music, and boot up the software. We get to compare all the toys that may look remarkably similar but often turn out to be quite different. For example, we put the toy trains together and find out which ones don't stay on the tracks.

How We're Different

The Oppenheim Toy Portfolio was founded in 1989 as the only independent consumer review of children's media. Unlike most other groups that rate products, we do not charge entry fees or accept ads from manufacturers. When you see our award seals on products, you can be assured that they are "award-winning" because they were selected by a noted expert in child development, children's literature, and education, and then rated by the most objective panel of judges—kids.

The Real Experts Speak:
Kids and Their Families

To get a meaningful sampling, we deal with families from all walks of life. We have testers in the city and in the country, in diapers and in blue jeans, in school clothes and in tutus. They have parents who are teachers, secretaries, lawyers, doctors, writers, engineers, doormen, software programmers, editors, psychologists, librarians, engineers, business people, architects, family therapists, musicians, artists, nurses, and early childhood educators. In some instances we have tested products in preschool and after-school settings where we can get feedback from groups of children. Since all new products tend to have novelty appeal, we ask our testers to live with a product for a while before assessing it. Among other things, we always ask—would you recommend it to others?

Criteria We Use for
Choosing Quality Products

- What is this product designed to do and how well does it do it?

- What can the child do with the product? Does it invite

active doing and thinking or simply passive watching?

- Is it safe and well-designed, and can it withstand the unexpected?

- Does it "fit" the developmental needs, interests, and typical skills of the children for whom it was designed?

- What message does it convey? Toys as well as books and videos can say a great deal about values parents are trying to convey. For example, does the product reflect old sexual stereotypes that limit children's views of themselves and others?

- What will a child learn from this product? Is it a "smart" product that will engage the child's mind or simply a novelty with limited play value?

- Is it entertaining? No product makes our list if kids find it boring, no matter how "good" or "educational" it claims to be.

- Is the age label correct? Is the product so easy that it will be boring or so challenging that it will be frustrating?

Rating System

Outstanding products, selected by our testers, are awarded one of four honors:

Platinum Award—These represent the most innovative, engaging new products of the year. See the 1999 Platinum Buying Guide.

Gold Seal Award—Given to outstanding new products that enhance the lives of children. All products selected for this book have received a Gold Seal Award unless they are marked "Mixed Emotions." Those products that receive a Gold Seal during the year are nominated for the year-end top Platinum Award List.

Blue Chip Classic Award—Reserved for classic products that should not be missed just because they weren't invented yesterday.

SNAP Award—Our Special Needs Adaptable Product Award is given to products that can be used by or easily adapted for children with special needs. All products reviewed in that chapter are recommended; the most outstanding are SNAP Award winners.

Using This Book

Each section begins with a play profile that tells you what to expect during each developmental stage and what "basic gear" will enhance learning and play. We also give you suggestions for best gifts for your budget and, perhaps most importantly, a stage-by-stage list of toys to avoid.

Because we know how busy people are these days, our reviews are purposely short and provide information on how to get your hands on the product.

A word about prices: Our award-winning products are not all high-ticket items. We have selected the very best products in toy supermarkets, as well as those that you will find in specialty stores, museum shops, and quality catalogs. We have listed the suggested retail prices, but they will vary tremendously depending on where you shop.

Telephone numbers: Where available, we have given a customer service number in case you have difficulty locating the product in your area.

Child's Play—More Than Fun!

For children, playing is more than a fun way to fill the day. It's through play that children learn and develop all sorts of important physical, intellectual, and social skills. Like musicians, children use well-chosen toys, books, and music to orchestrate their play. As they grow and develop, so does their need for more complex playthings that challenge and enhance their learning. Toys and stories with the right developmental fit help create a marvelous harmony for learning and fun. **The Oppenheim Toy Portfolio** is a resource book you can use to make that kind of mix.

1999 Platinum Buying Guide

1999 PLATINUM TOY AWARDS

INFANTS

Sensational Circus Musical Mobile (Manhattan Toy)
Flatso Farm Musical Pull Down* (North American Bear)/**Slumbertime Soother*** (Fisher-Price)
Early E. Bird (International Playthings)
Puzzle Cube (Wimmer-Ferguson)
Fascination Station (Sassy)

TODDLERS

Activity Table (Fisher-Price)

Duplo School Bus (Lego Systems)

Groovy Girls Dolls (Manhattan Toy)

Miss Spider Pull Toy (Learning Curve)

Yum Yum Cookie Monster* (Tyco)/
Elmo & His Pet Puppy* (Tyco)

PRESCHOOLERS

Barney Song Magic Banjo (Playskool)

Fire Engine for Two (Step 2)

Goodnight Moon Game (Briarpatch)

9-in-1 Easel (Little Tikes)

Sassafras Bear (Manhattan Toy)

Shop 'n' Cook Kitchen (Fisher-Price)

*indicates a tie in the category

1999 PLATINUM TOY AWARDS

EARLY SCHOOL YEARS

Puppets & Dolls

Finger Puppet Theater & Stylish Steppers
  (Manhattan Toy)

Muffy VanderBear Pagoda Collection with tea set*
  (North American Bear)/**Les Mini Corolline*** (Corolle)

Vehicles

Celestial Stinger (Lego Systems)

Cyclone X-V Racers (Mattel)

Rokenbok Expandable RC Building System
  (Rokenbok)

Tyco Revolver RC Stunt Vehicle (Mattel)

Games & Crafts

Round the Bend (International Playthings)

GeoSafari Talking Globe Jr. (Educational Insights)

Flower Crazy Desk Set (Learning Curve)

Hand painted Ceramic Piggy Bank (Creativity for Kids)

My Art Gallery (Alex)

National Geographic: Mola Pillow (Curiosity Kits)

*indicates a tie in a category

1999 PLATINUM BOOK AWARDS

INFANTS AND TODDLERS

Old MacDonald and **The Itsy-Bitsy Spider** (Wells, Scholastic)

Peek-A-Moo and **Row, Row, Row Your Goat** (Most, Harcourt Brace)

Cows In the Kitchen (Crebbin/McEwen, Candlewick)

Good Night, Baby Bear (Asch, Harcourt Brace)

I Love You Just the Way You Are (Miller, Candlewick)

When Mama Comes Home Tonight (Spinelli/Dyer, Simon & Schuster)

You're Just What I Need (Krauss/Noonan, HarperCollins)

PRESCHOOLERS

The Flying Garbanzos (Saltzberg, Crown)

If You Give A Pig a Pancake (Numeroff/Bond, HarperCollins)

What Baby Wants (Root/Barton, Candlewick)

What Mommies Do Best/What Daddies Do Best (Numeroff/Munsinger, Simon & Schuster)

Who Hops? (Davis, Harcourt Brace)

EARLY SCHOOL YEARS

Fishing for Methuselah (Roth, HarperCollins)

Hooray for Diffendoofer Day! (Seuss, Prelutsky/Smith, Knopf)

The Lost and Found (Teague, Scholastic)

Money Troubles (Cosby/Honeywood, Scholastic)

The New Way Things Work (Macaulay, Houghton Mifflin)

Optical Tricks (Wick, Scholastic)

Out of This World/Seeing Stars (Stott/Muirden, Candlewick)

Raising Dragons (Nolen/Primavera, Harcourt Brace)

The Secret Knowledge of Grown-Ups (Wisniewski, Lothrop)

Willy the Dreamer (Browne, Candlewick)

You Can Make a Collage (Carle, Klutz)

You Can't Take a Balloon Into the Metropolitan Museum (Weitzman & Glasser, Dial)

1999 PLATINUM VIDEO AWARDS

PRESCHOOLERS

Big Bird Gets Lost (Sony)

Blue's Clues Story Time (Paramount)

Goodnight, Little Bear (Paramount)

EARLY SCHOOL YEARS

The Big Space Shuttle (Little Mammoth Media)

The Borrowers (Polygram)

Fairy Tale (Paramount)

Global Friends of Japan (Global Friends)

The Lion King II: Simba's Pride (Disney)

Madeline (TriStar)

The Magic School Bus: Getting Energized (Kid Vision)

Oliver Twist (Disney)

Where Does My Garbage Go? (Middlemarch)

1999 PLATINUM AUDIO AWARDS

MUSIC

40 Winks (Harper, Alacazam!)

Elmopalooza (Sony)

Friends Forever (Disney)

Singin' at the Swing Set (Kid'n Together)

Songs From a Parent to a Child (Sony)

Sounds Familiar (D&A Records)

Peter, Paul & Mary Around the Campfire (Warner Bros.)

The Lion King: Original Broadway Cast (Disney)

The Mozart Effect Vols.1–3 (BMG)

STORIES

Arthur's New Puppy (Brown, Little, Brown)

The Illustrated Book of Ballet Stories (Newman/Tomblin, DK)

My Father's Dragon (Gannett, Listening Library)

Tell Me About the Night I Was Born (Curtis, Harper Audio)

Zap (Edmark)

Nintendo Gameboy Camera & Printer (Nintendo)

Encarta Reference Suite (Microsoft)

World Book Encyclopedia 98 (IBM)

Due to the late release dates of children's software, the complete 1999 Platinum Software List will be posted on our website, www.toyportfolio.com.

Activity Table (Fisher-Price)

Barney Song Magic Banjo (Playskool)

Dunk & Clunk Rings (Sassy)

Elmo & His Pet Puppy (Tyco)

Follow the Lights Talking Phone (Mattel)

Hug & Learn Little Leap (Leapfrog)

Puzzle Cube * (Wimmer-Ferguson) / **Sort'n'Go Car*** (VTech)

Round Carousel Bells (Battat)

Pippy Pals Dress Up * (Pamela Drake) / **FeltKids Design Kits*** (Learning Curves)

Slumbertime Soother (Fisher-Price)

Threading Cheese & Apple (Learning Curve)

Kids are by nature social beings, and enjoy few things more than being with other kids. Still, learning to share and play together can be rough going. We kept an eye out this year for toys that work especially well with groups of kids. For kids who are still at the "it's mine" stage, the key is to find toys with enough multiple pieces to go around. We also looked for products that lend themselves to cooperative play—whether it's a board game or activity kit that more than one child can enjoy together or simply side by side. We often talk these days about interactive toys, but here are some wonderful products for interactive kids.

Creativity Street (Chenille Craft)

Duplo School Bus (Lego System)

Giant Castle Sand Set (Battat)

FeltKids Design Kits (Learning Curve)

Round the Bend (International Playthings)

Preschool Puppet Kit (Creativity for Kids)

Puppet Stages (Alex/Creative Ed. of Canada)

Rokenbok Expandable RC Building System (Rokenbok)

Shop & Cook Kitchen (Fisher-Price)

Toobers & Zots Flowers (HandsOn)

Whether your kids are getting top grades or the other kind, there are playful ways you can help. Here are some of our highlighted favorites that give school skills a boost without having to break out the flashcards.

Alphabet & Phonics
Hug & Learn Little Leap (Leap Frog)
New A to Z Panels Puzzles (Lauri)

Storytelling & Language
I Spy Preschool Game (Briarpatch)
Illustory Kit (Chimeric)
Easel & art supplies
Puppet & puppet stages

Prewriting Skills
Peg Bead Kits (Hama)
Lacing Games (Lauri, Learning Curve)
Lite Brite (Hasbro)
Sewing Kits (Quincrafts, Curiosity Kits)
Collage-a-Family (Alex)

Math Skills
Aliens (Gamewright)
Lego Mindstorms (Lego Systems)
Mad Math Game (Patrick)
Math Magic Machine (Chicco)
Sum Swamp Game (Learning Resources)
Twist & Shout Addition (Leap Frog)
Unifix Cubes (Didax)

TOP-RATED OFFICE TOYS '99

Whether your office is in a complex or in a corner of your home, when kids come to visit, having a few quiet toys can make the time more enjoyable for everyone. Besides a pack of crayons and paper, here are some top choices:

Toddler/Preschooler

Lego Primo (Lego Systems)

Little People Playhouse (Fisher-Price)

3-in-1 Portable Art Studio (Fisher-Price)

Magna Doodle (Fisher-Price)

Pippy Pals (Pamela Drake)

Early School Years

Free Style Lego Table or Bucket (Lego Systems)

Gears & Gizmos (Learning Resources)

Lite Brite (Hasbro)

Puzzles, Parquetry Blocks & Patterns

Tape Player with volume lock & headphones

Begin to Sew kits (Quincrafts)

Stormy Seas (Binary Art)

Connections (Tiger)

Although parents are generally busier than ever, many of the best toys for preschoolers and school-aged kids this season seem to be very adult intensive. Elaborate construction kits labeled for ages 8–12 are often far too complex for beginners to tackle solo. The problem is not with your child, but with the age labels. Similarly, there are craft kits that involve using microwave ovens, sewing with needles, hammering with real tools, plugging into the VCR or mixing up papier mache. Without taking over, adults can help kids get started and be there as a "consultant," giving kids strategies for working in an orderly fashion.

Sure, there are lots of great toys that kids can use alone, but cooperative projects provide the raw materials for interactions that can be rewarding for adult and child. Making time to do such things together gives you a chance to play and experiment together – a chance to solve problems, think creatively and even have fun learning together. Here are some of our favorites:

Goodnight Moon Game (Briarpatch)

FeltKids Interactive Books (Learning Curve)

Geosafari Jr. Talking Globe (Educational Insights)

Handpainted Piggy Bank (Creativity for Kids)

Lego Mindstorms (Lego Systems)

National Geographic: My World Quilt (Curiosity Kit)

Rokenbok Expandable RC Building System (Rokenbok)

Super Zooom Balls (Curiosity Kits)

Many of the toys, books, and videos you bring home may have a built-in Gender Agenda™—products that reinforce stereotypes and shape your child's self-image. It often begins innocently in the nursery with pastel color coding, but quickly moves on to a glut of products with themes of hairplay for girls and gunplay for boys. The gender issue is not just one that is important to girls. The overly aggressive and violent-themed toys and video games directed at boys are even more alarming to us than the dating games or lavendar blocks that come with blueprints for a shopping mall.

Can you avoid all gender-specific toys? Probably not. These are often the products kids want the most, not only because they are heavily promoted on TV, but also because children tend to sort the world out in the simple and absolute terms of right or wrong, hard or easy, boy or girl. There are, however, positive choices you can make—where a gender-free product will work for both boys and girls... and products that break gender stereotypes.

Big Bulldozer Giant Puzzle (Frank Schaffer)

Community Worker Costumes (Small World)

Fire Engine for Two (Step 2)

Glockenspiel Kit (Woodstock Percussion)

Homecrafted Toys (Homecrafters)

Jumbo Trike (Kettler)

Lunar Activity Kit (Great Explorations)

Paint the Wild Kits (Balitono)

Thumb Ball (Saturnian 1)

WNBA Barbie (Mattel)

TOP-RATED MULTICULTURAL PRODUCTS '99

Many new products reflect our cultural diversity. What do we mean by multicultural? Some products introduce kids to cultures beyond their own and expand their view of the world. Others reflect more familiar settings. The best of these products capture our differences along with the universal feelings that connect us.

Toys

Djembe Drum (Remo/Woodstock)

Asian Dolls (Global Friends)

Glockenspiel Kit (Woodstock)

Josefina (Pleasant Company)

National Geographic: Mola Kit (Curiosity Kits)

TOP RATED TOYS: $20 OR UNDER '99

These are just a few of the many items for $20 or under that will make a big hit for birthday parties or a "just because" gift.

Infants and toddlers

Early E. Bird (International Playthings)

Turtle Tower (Sassy)

Stack 'n' Build Choo Choo (Fisher-Price)

Puzzle Cube (Wimmer-Ferguson)

Preschoolers and Early School Years

Construction Truck & Hat (Little Tikes)

Create Your Own Scrapbook (Creativity for Kids)

I Spy Floor Puzzle or **Statue of Libery Puzzle** (Briarpatch/Frank Schaffer)

Lego Freestyle Building Table (Lego Systems)

Mini Corolline (Corolle)

Radio Watch (Wild Planet)

X-V Racers (Mattel)

BEST BATTERY-OPERATED TOYS '99

Every year we test dozens of toys that run on batteries. Some lose their interest before the batteries run out. That's why battery toys often get a bad rap. In looking at our Platinum and Gold winners over the years, however, we realized that a surprising number of vehicles and building toys as well as music and learning game machines run on batteries. Many of the best are variations of classics—with the added bells and whistles that batteries can provide. For kids with special needs, the lights, sounds, and motion of such toys are a plus that provides sensory feedback and greater independence.

INFANTS , TODDLERS & PRESCHOOLERS

Slumbertime Soother (Fisher-Price)

Elmo & his Pet Puppy* / Yum Yum Cookie Monster* (Tyco)

Sort 'n' Go Car (VTech)

Follow-the-Lights Talking Phone (Mattel)

Song Magic Banjo (Playskool)

Musical Cake Surprise (Fisher-Price)

Hug & Learn Little Leap (Leapfrog)

EARLY SCHOOL YEARS

Knock Knock Mr. Potato Head (Playskool)

GeoSafari Talking Junior Globe (Educational Insights)

Little Smart Super Sound Works Keyboard (VTech)

Tyco Revolver RC Stunt Vehicle (Mattel)

X-V Racers Cyclone (Mattel)

8 & up

Celestial Stinger (Lego)

Connections (Tiger)

Rokenbok Expandable RC Building System (Rokenbok)

*indicates a tie in a category

All battery-operated toys tested with Energizer brand batteries.

1 • Infants
Birth to One Year

What to Expect Developmentally

Learning Through the Senses. Right from the start, babies begin learning by looking, listening, touching, smelling, and tasting. It's through their senses that they make sense of the world. In this first remarkable year, babies progress from gazing to grasping, from touching to tossing, from watching to doing. By selecting a rich variety of playthings, parents can match their baby's sensory learning style.

Reaching Out. Initially, you will be the one to activate the mobile, shake the rattle, squeeze the squeaker. But before long, baby will be reaching out and taking hold of things and engaging you in a game of peekaboo.

Toys and Development. As babies develop, so do their needs for playthings that fit their growing abilities. Like clothes, good toys need to fit. Some of the toys for newborns will have short-term use and then get packed away or passed along to a new cousin or friend. Others, such as the crib-rail activity center, may become a favorite floor toy. Still others will be used in new ways. During this first year, babies need toys to gaze at, listen to, grasp, chomp on, shake, pass from one hand to another, bang together, toss, chase, and hug.

1

Your Role in Play. No baby needs all the toys listed here. In fact, to your new baby, no toy will be more interesting than your smiling face, the sound of your voice, and the touch of your hands. Playing with your baby is not just fun—it's one of the most important ways babies learn about themselves and the world of people and things!

The Horizontal Infant

Time was when infants' rooms and products were all pastel. Not any more—research has shown that during the early weeks of life babies respond to the sharp contrast of black-and-white patterns. But does that mean your whole nursery needs to be black and white? Not at all. In no time, your baby is going to be responding to bright colors, interesting sounds, and motion.

BASIC GEAR CHECKLIST
FOR THE HORIZONTAL INFANT

✓ Mobile
✓ Musical toys
✓ Crib mirror
✓ Soft fabric toys with differing sounds and textures
✓ Fabric dolls or animals with easy-to-grab limbs
✓ Activity mat

Toys to Avoid

These toys pose choking and/or suffocation hazards:

✓ Antique rattles
✓ Foam toys
✓ Toys with elastic
✓ Toys with buttons, bells, and ribbons
✓ Old wooden toys that may contain lead paint
✓ Furry plush dolls that shed
✓ Any toys with small parts

These toys are developmentally inappropriate:

✓ Shape sorters and ring-and-post toys, which call for skills that are beyond infants

Crib Toys
Musical Toys, Mobiles, Mirrors, and More Musical Toys

Few toys are as soothing to newborns as a music box with its quiet sounds. Today, most musical toys for infants don't come as boxes but as plush toys. We prefer some of the newer pull-down musicals to soft plush dolls with hard metal wind-up keys that older babies may chew or get poked with by accident. When baby starts turning over, use musical wind-up plush dolls with supervision, not as crib toys.

■ Flatso Farm Musical Pulldown 🏆 PLATINUM AWARD

(North American Bear $36) Framed in a soft red barn, sheep, duck, and cow watch a wiggly piglet ride up to the tune of "Old MacDonald." Bring home with soft velour **Flatso Rattles** ($10), with eye-catching patterned bodies and gentle sounds. This company's Platinum Award-winning **Crib Notes Watering Can** ($36), with a friendly spider hanging down from the green and pink velour watering can, plays "Eensy Weensy Spider." (800) 682-3427.

■ Inchworm Pull Musical 🏆

(Manhattan Baby $20) Pull the small sunflower and it travels upwards to the red smiling faced Inchworm as it plays "You Are My Sunshine" Or, still charming, the **Enchanted Garden Sunflower Pull Musical,** a smiley yellow sunflower for baby's crib with a perky bug that rides the long green stem inching up as it plays "Beautiful Dreamer." Platinum Award '97. (800) 747-2454.

■ Slumbertime Soother 🏆 PLATINUM AWARD

(Fisher-Price $34.99) Everyone's been there—the baby is almost asleep but the music has stopped. If you walk into the room to turn it back on, you start the whole process over again. To the rescue—an innovative remote-controlled musical toy that can be restarted from 20 feet. Has lights that change with the music, or nature sounds. Plays 10 lullabies that can be adjusted for volume (a plus). Takes 4 C and 2 AA batteries. Also looked promising but not ready for testing, **Kick & Play Piano** 🏆 (Fisher-Price $24.99). Babies activate this innovative musical and light-up crib toy by kicking the soft key pad. Converts to a floor toy. Requires 3 AA batteries. (800) 435-5437.

■ Windup Puppy 🏅

(North American Bear $25) A cheerful looking black-and-white puppy of soft jersey has a music box (removable so the pup can be bathed) that plays "Where Has My Little Dog Gone?" Perfect for gazing at as infants fall asleep. (800) 682-3427.

NOTABLE PREVIOUS WINNERS:

Classical Pooh Pullstring Musical (Gund $25) We still love last year's Platinum Award winner Pooh, who's holding on to a big red balloon—in search of honey, of course! (732) 248-1500. **Peter Rabbit Musical Pillow** BLUE CHIP (Eden $20) Tie this 8" musical pillow embroidered with Peter Rabbit onto a newborn's bassinet, crib, or stroller. A small, comforting take-along for trips away from home. (800) 443-4275.

SAFETY TIP: Pillows and stuffed animals left in cribs present a suffocation hazard.

Mobiles

A musical mobile attached to crib rail or changing table provides baby with fascinating sights and sounds. During the first three months, infants can focus only on objects that are relatively close. Toys should be between 8" and 14" from their eyes. Before you buy any mobile, look at it from the baby's perspective. What can you see? Many attractive mobiles are purely for decoration and do not have images that face the baby in the crib. Here are our favorites:

■ Sensational Circus Musical Mobile 🏅 PLATINUM AWARD

(Manhattan Baby $40) Baby can watch these bright eye-grabbers as they spin. Newest from an appealing series of mobiles with different themes. Also recommended, **Merry Meadows** or the **Sunflower Enchanted Garden.** Designed from the horizontal baby's perspective with faces smiling down at baby. All play Brahms' "Lullabye." (800) 747-2454.

■ Flatso Farm Mobile ⭐99⭐

(North American Bear $54) A companion piece to the **Flatso Farm Pull Musical,** this charming mobile has a cow, duck, pig, and lamb dangling from a red barn. Plays "Farmer in the Dell." Very special. (800) 682-3427.

■ Infant Stim-Mobile BLUE CHIP

(Wimmer-Ferguson $20) New baby will be fascinated with the black-and-white, high-contrast patterns of the ten vinyl 3" discs and squares that dance and dangle on this nonmusical mobile for the crib or changing table. May not look as cute as other mobiles, but babies do react to the visual stimulation of this early crib toy. (800) 747-2454.

■ Panda Domino Mobile BLUE CHIP

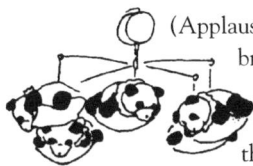

(Applause/Dakin $50) Black-and-white pandas with bright collars around their necks spin to the tune of "Twinkle, Twinkle, Little Star." A consistent winner with infants, who enjoy the sounds, sights, and motion, and parents who want something decorative as well as functional. Platinum Award '93. (800) 777-6990.

> **SAFETY TIP: Mobiles should be removed by the time baby is five months, or whenever she can reach out and touch them, to avoid the danger of strangulation or choking on small parts.**

Mirrors and More

■ Double-Feature Crib Mirror BLUE CHIP

(Wimmer-Ferguson $34) A truly distortion-free crib mirror. Comes with mirror on one side and high-contrast graphics, including a face and a boat, on the other side; the latter will be of greatest interest to younger babies. Unlike many crib toys, this mirror ties at all four corners, so it can't be used as a lift-and-bang toy like many other crib mirrors. (800) 747-2454.

■ Crib Center BLUE CHIP

(Little Tikes $20) Baby can begin to investigate nine different activities on this bright yellow combination crib mirror/activity center, which can be used later as a carry-about toy. The spinner and color wheel provide early lessons in cause and effect. One toy tester family raved that this toy bought them an extra 20 minutes of sleep in the morning! (800) 321-0183.

> **SAFETY TIP: Be sure to check toys with Velcro patches for sharp edges that can scratch.**

■ Earlyears Activity Shapes ⭐99

(International Playthings $13) Brightly colored shapes and patterns dangling from a soft blue triangle that crinkle, rattle, and squeak. Attaches with Velcro fastener to crib, stroller, or car seat. A good gazing toy for the early months that your baby can safely reach out to touch. (800) 445-8347.

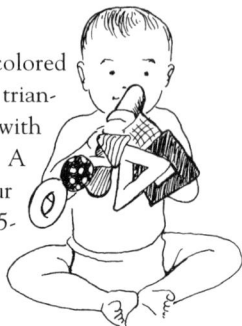

Equipment for Playtime

Best in Its Category:

■ Funtime Soft Bouncer Seat

(Summer Infant $50) This fabric chair provides the perfect perspective for young infants who are ready for a little elevation but are not able to sit up. Comes with spinning toys on a bar that baby will first gaze at and later activate. Use with adult supervision only. Up to 25 pounds. (800) 268-6237.

> **SAFETY TIP: Never place any type of baby carrier on a table, bed, or counter. Even though the baby has never done it before, there's no way of predicting when he will make a move that can tip the carrier.**

■ Deluxe Gymini 3-D Activity Gym ⭐99

(Tiny Loves $39.95–50) Gyms with dangly toys to swipe at are enjoyed for a short period of time. This soft version, a play mat with two arches, got high marks for keeping baby entertained. Also available in high-contrast black, white, and red version. Not for babies who are beginning to pull themselves up. New deluxe version is slightly larger. (800) 843-6292. Plastic gyms have gotten mixed reports. Older babies have gotten feet caught and even kicked a few over. Our caution remains with any gym you use—total supervision is required.

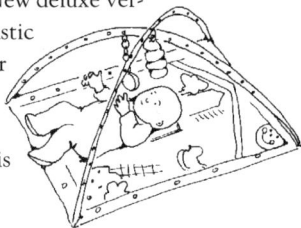

> **SAFETY TIP: Many parents find the back-and-forth action of a swing a soothing diversion for a restless infant. However, we find it difficult to recommend any infant swings because they can entrap limbs and necks or even collapse. If you choose to use one, we urge you not to leave the room. Use it with constant supervision.**

First Lap and Floor Toys:
Rattles, Sound Toys, and More

Infant toys can help adults engage and interact with newborns. A bright rattle that baby tracks visually, a quiet music box that soothes, or an interesting doll to gaze or swipe at are ideal for beginning getting-acquainted games. These toys can be used at the changing table or for lap games during playful moments after a feeding, before a bath, or whenever.

■ Flip'n'Play Mirror

(Fisher-Price $6.99) Star-shaped points of bold black-and-white patterns circle this hand held mirror. Flip it over and the points now are in color and have interesting textures that circle a smiling face that lifts and flips to reveal a yellow peek-a-boo face. Add a shake and it rattles. So much sensory input for one little toy! Birth & up. (800) 432-KIDS.

■ Lamaze's First Mirror

(Learning Curve $19.99) A fabric-covered wedge with a mirror for baby to peer into and covered in eye-grabbing bold black & white patterns with red piping. The mirror in a soft fabric frame can be removed and used separately. Platinum Award '98. (800) 704-8697.

■ **Lamaze Peek-a-boo Puppet**

(Learning Curve $15) Here's a reversible puppet that changes from a black-and-white spotted bunny to a green turtle with a checkered back and a squeaker in its head. Fun for early tracking, talking, and peek-a-boo games. New for '99, **Wild and Woolly Puppet** looked promising but was not ready for testing. (800) 704-8697.

Q **ACTIVITY TIP: There are few things more important to your child's development than talking. For adults who feel uncomfortable talking, singing, or conversing with newborns, a puppet may give them the security of a prop. If you're rusty with your nursery rhymes and baby games, see the book section for parent resources.**

■ **The Nursery Novel**

(Wimmer-Ferguson $12) An eye-grabbing page-turner to share with your early "reader." Eight vivid fabric panels can fold like an accordion or open into a long, long panel with bold graphics, a peek-a-boo mirror, and satin ribbons to feel at either end. Nice for lap time sharing, turning, focusing, talking, and touching. (800) 747-2454.

■ **Visual Cards** 💰

(Sassy $6.99) New babies will enjoy gazing at these two cards with high contrast images and licks of primary colors on all four sides. Flip them for a change of visual interest from time to time as they stand on the changing table or in the crib, or enjoy as a book for lap time. One side has a mirror, another a smiling face, a spiral pattern, and a puppy's face. Birth & up. (800) 323-6336.

Rattles

Many rattles are too noisy, hard, and heavy for newborns. While most will be used by adults to get baby's attention, the best choices for newborns are rattles with a soft sound that won't startle and a soft finish that won't hurt. During the first months, an infant's arm and hand movements are not yet refined. Here are some of the best rattles for early playtimes:

■ Baby's First Silly Sounds BLUE CHIP

(Gund $8–$25) Each of these chubby ball-shaped toys has its own sound that will attract baby's attention. They can be joined together by Velcro tabs on arms. Available with farm animals or Winnie-the-Pooh characters. Also top-rated, **Linky Dink Geometrics** ($9). Three interlocked velour shapes have a quiet rattle stitched inside, excellent for two-handed play. (732) 248-1500.

■ Elephant Sensory Teether

(Manhattan Baby $9) Teethers will eventually find and appreciate the soft, chewy teether on an adorable little red velour elephant with purple ears and rattle inside. But for now it's soft and safe for batting at and tracking. Also charming, a bright yellow and blue **Bear Sensory Teether** and their orange and yellow **Monkey Ring Rattle.** Infants & up. (800) 747-2454.

■ Little Lessons Turtle

(Eden $12) So much to see and hear with this little turtle that has easy-to-grab loop feet, a see-through squeaky textured shell with balls inside that spin around, and a black-and-white spiral on its underside. (800) 443-4275.

Q ACTIVITY TIP: Play "Buzzing Bees." Hold your fist in the air and say, "Here is a beehive, but where are the bees? Hiding inside—watch and see!" Wiggle your fingers and make buzzing sounds as you gently tickle the baby.

■ Rainbow Bear

(Gund $10) A cheerful velour bear with a rattle inside is done in primary colors and comes with all stitched features. Small babies will enjoy gazing at him and eventually reaching out to touch and taste. Also recommended, **Fwoggy** (Gund $10), a jolly-looking spotted velour frog with jingle sound and easy-to-grab legs, each with bright licks of color. (732) 248-1500.

■ Sunflower Toy

(Manhattan Baby $13) Squeeze the petals of this smiling velour sunflower for squeak, rattle, and crinkle sounds. Shake it for a jolly jingle. Pretty and interesting for early sensory exploration. Hand washable. Newborn & up. (800) 747-2454.

■ Tinkle, Crinkle, Rattle, & Squeak

(Gund $10) Like the original caterpillar-shaped toy with multiple sounds and bright primary colors, this update is done in black and white with licks and checked patterns for eye grabbing attention. The long slender shape is easy for baby to eventually grab hold of and explore. (732) 248-1500.

The Vertical Infant

Many of the toys from the horizontal stage will still be used. By now, however, the mobile should be removed from the crib, and new, interesting playthings should be added gradually. As new toys are introduced, put some of the older things away. Recycle toys that have lost their novelty by putting them out of sight for a while; then reintroduce them or give them away. A clutter of playthings can become more of a distraction than an attraction.

⚙ BASIC GEAR CHECKLIST FOR THE VERTICAL INFANT

✓ Rattles and teething toys
✓ Manipulatives with differing shapes, sounds, textures
✓ Washable dolls and animals
✓ Musical toys
✓ Soft fabric-covered ball
✓ Rolling toys or vehicles
✓ Plastic containers for filling and dumping games
✓ Cloth blocks
✓ Bath toys
✓ Cloth or sturdy cardboard books

🚫 Toys to Avoid

These toys pose choking and/or suffocation hazards:

✓ Antique rattles
✓ Foam toys
✓ Toys with elastic
✓ Toys with buttons, bells, and ribbons
✓ Old wooden toys that may contain lead paint
✓ Furry plush dolls that shed
✓ Any toys with small parts

These toys are developmentally inappropriate:

✓ Shape sorters and ring-and-post toys call for skills that are beyond infants.

Rattles and Teethers

Now is the time for manipulatives that encourage two-handed exploration as well as provide interesting textures, sounds, and safe, chewable surfaces for teething.

■ Baby Smiley Face Rattle

(Sassy $7.50) A smiling face with jiggly eyes, squeaky nose button, rolling beads, and chewy polka-dotted handle-shaped ears reverses for a peek at baby's own smiling face in a distortion-free mirror. (800) 323-6336.

■ Birdy Tweeter 🏆

(Ambi $10) Shake the little blue bird and it quietly tweets. Easy-to-grasp yellow handle invites baby to discover first small lessons in cause and effect. Also highly recommended from the same line, the **Funshine Mirror** (BLUE CHIP) and **Twin Rattle**. (310) 645-9680.

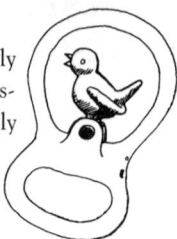

■ Earlyears Earl E. Bird 🏆
PLATINUM AWARD

(International Playthings $12) Soft and interesting textures and patterns make this easy-to-grab "bird" a good choice for newborns and beyond. There's something for all the senses on this colorful toy with crinkle and squeak sounds as well as chewable rings for teething. Birth & up. Also highly recommended for teething from the same line, **Chewing Rings** ($9.95). (800) 445-8347.

■ Lamaze Clack Rattle 🏆

(Learning Curve $6.99) Easy to grasp, this two-handled circle has two clackers that make a clacking sound and move when baby shakes the vivid primary colored rattle. Red on one side, yellow on the other, this is good for two handed play. 3 months & up. Also recommended, **Lamaze Rattlebug** ($8) with chewy wings that are easy to grasp and soothing for teethers. (800) 432-5437.

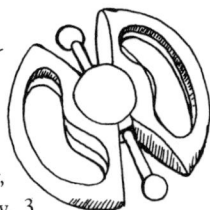

■ Tolo Deluxe Rattle 🏆

(Small World $ 4) Three colorful bars spin and rattle and respond to the touch of a finger. Good for two-handed play and single-digit action. (310) 645-9680.

Floor Toys

First Blocks

■ Earlyears Pyramid Clutch 🏆

(International Playthings $13) This easy-to-grab toy will appeal to all of your baby's senses and develop two-handed play. It has great textures on the handles and a rattle safely inside

the triangle center shape, and our babies loved to taste it! (800) 445-8347. Still wonderful with the same features but in a cube shape, Learning Curve's **Lamaze Clutch Cube** ($12). (800) 704-8697.

■ Mind Shapes

(Wimmer-Ferguson $20) Three fabric shapes (ball, cube, and pyramid) to shake, toss, and touch for sensory exploration. Each with a distinctive sound, vivid black-and-white patterns, as well as bright primary colors and interesting textures. Ideal for attracting baby's visual attention for focusing and tracking. Platinum Award '97. (800) 747-2454.

Q **ACTIVITY TIP: Make a stack of soft blocks and give baby a demo in knocking them down. Encourage baby to do an instant replay. Provide "boom diddy boom" sound effects!**

Filling and Spilling Games

With their newly acquired skills of grasping and letting go comes the favorite game of filling and dumping multiple objects in and out of containers.

■ Baby's First Blocks and Snap Lock Beads BLUE CHIP

(Fisher-Price $8 & $3.99) Babies will enjoy these toys long before they can do what the boxes promise. **Baby's First Blocks** is technically a shape-sorter, but the 12 blocks will be used to fill, spill, and throw long before baby can fit them into the three-place shape-sorter lid of the container. Put the lid away for now. Long before baby can pull the lemon-sized **Snap-Lock** plastic beads apart or put them together, they'll be used for chomping on, picking up, tossing, and little games of fill and dump. Great for developing fine motor skills and the ability to litter the floor. (800) 432-5437.

■ Dunk & Clunk Circus Rings

(Sassy $8.50) Multi-textured rings and rattles slip into special slots in the lid of this see-through container. Beginners will like tasting, tossing, and dropping pieces into the plastic box with polka-dotted handle, but older tots will like this unusual shape sorter that develops fine tuning of wrist and finger action. 9 mos. & up. (800) 323-6336.

Q ACTIVITY TIP: Put five or six interesting small toys and baby books in a paper bag or box for baby to explore. This is one way to help baby establish short independent playtimes. Small boxes with toys inside motivate exploration and make happy surprises.

■ Primo Storage Ladybug 💇

(Lego Primo $10) A see-through tub with red ladybug top holds a colorful assortment of big chunky plastic blocks that are ideal for grasping, filling, spilling, and eventually stacking. A slightly larger container includes a wheeled base that can be used for stacking and rolling back and forth. Also fun, a three-piece add-on **Squeak & Rrrattle** set ($5) with flower-shaped squeaker and splat-shaped smiling rattle that looks perfect for teethers. (800) 233-8756.

■ Puzzle Cube 💇 PLATINUM AWARD

(Wimmer-Ferguson $16) A fabric cube of black-&-white high contrast graphics reverses to bold primary patterns. A crinkle crescent, squeaker star, and rattle heart with interesting textures and sounds fit into cut-out openings on the cube. Unlike shape sorters for older tots, these soft shapes fit into any opening. 6 mos. & up. Also interesting, **Stacking Cubes** 💇 ($20), a three-piece patterned fabric cube set that includes a rattle block that fits inside a larger block that fits inside another slightly larger block. Baby will not be able to nest the cube & small open block, but these are fun for parent/child games. 6 mos. & up. (800) 747-2454.

Toys for Making Things Happen

Some of the best infant toys introduce babies to their first lessons in cause and effect. Such toys respond with sounds or motion that give even the youngest players a sense of "can do" power—of making things happen!

■ Baby Laptop

(Little Tikes $18) An activity toy for the '90s with plenty of buttons to push. Lift-up screen has a mirror for peek-a-boo fun. Lights and music gave testers early lessons in cause and effect. Battery operated. 6 mos. & up. Platinum Award '98. (800) 321-0183.

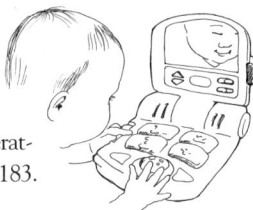

■ Earlyears Floor Spinner

(International Playthings $14.95) There are plenty of sights and sounds to explore as baby turns and manipulates this intriguing floor toy. Each of the four cones has a distinctive activity: beads, beeper, mirror, and tracking ball. Ideal for two-handed play and fun for crawling babies to bat at and chase after. Platinum Award '95. (800) 445-8347.

■ Photo-Go-Round 🌟99🌟

(Fisher-Price $9.99) A peek-a-boo spinning toy you can personalize with photos of people significant to baby. It spins and has windows to open for peek-a-boo fun. Easy to carry to daycare or other places where having pictures of family can make separation easier. 8 mos. & up. (800) 432-5437.

■ Rolly Cow 🌟99🌟

(Learning Curve $14.99) A swipe of the hand will set this happy-looking cow bobbing and beads twirling. Satin ears and face make this furry critter a good choice for baby to hear, see, and touch. (800) 704-8697. Also charming, **Frog Chime Ball** (Manhattan Baby $15), a soft velour frog with stitched features sits on top of a chime ball. Neither of these will roll away from babies who are not crawling yet. (800) 747-2454.

■ Stack'n'Build Buddy 🌟99🌟

(Fisher-Price $8) There is no right or wrong way to stack the chunky blocks on top of Buddy's wobbly big feet. Buddy tips from side to side as pieces are added. His big yellow head with googlie eyes can be topped with a bright red cap. Babies will like knocking this over before they get the hang of stacking. A good floor toy for parent and child time. 8 mos. & up. (800) 432-5437.

■ Shake'n'Rattle Jack 🌟99🌟

(Playskool $6.99) Safely enclosed beads tumble through this oversized see-through blue jack. A good choice for two-handed play. (800) 233-8756. 6 mos. & up.

■ Shake 'n Roll Surprise 🌟99

(Lego Primo $4.99) We had trouble leaving this shiny red ball alone. Push the six colorful knobs with faces on this slick red ball and another face pops out on the other side. A good choice for early social games of roly-poly and peek-a-boo surprises. Fun for two-handed solo play and for learning about cause and effect. 3 mos. & up. (800) 233-8756.

■ Pop'n'Spin Top BLUE CHIP

(Playskool $13) An easy-to-activate top with big, colorful hopping-popping balls and a barbershop-like post that twirls inside a see-through dome. Baby just pushes a big red button to activate. Very satisfying toy for a baby who is just discovering the fun of making things happen. (800) 752-9755.

Best Highchair Toys 🌟99

Good highchair toys buy a few extra minutes before dinner is ready or allow you to eat, too! This year's best is **Fascination Station** 🌟99 **PLATINUM AWARD** *(Sassy $7.99) Our little tester had fun batting at this spinning toy that attaches to a tabletop with a stout suction cup that has a wobbly platform. There is plenty to see, hear, and feel as the balls and clackers with bold graphics and textures turn. What a surprise to discover that the spinner detaches to become a hand-held toy to explore! 6 months & up. (800) 323-6336. Previous winners:* **Earlyears Activity Spiral** *(International Playthings $14.95) comes with three activity balls that spin, squeak, and go clickity-clack! All of the balls spin up and down on an axle that is topped with a convex mirror for little games of peeka-boo. (800) 445-8347.* **Rota Rattle** *(Ambi $15): The youngest testers were able to make this updated classic work with a swipe of the hand. (301) 645-9680.*

First Toys for Crawlers

Rolling toys such as small vehicles and balls can match baby's developing mobility. Toys placed slightly beyond baby's reach can provide the motivation to get moving. But make it fun. Avoid turning this into a teasing time. Your object is to motivate, not frustrate. Games of rolling a ball or car back and forth make for happy social play between baby and older kids as well as adults.

■ Baby's First Car BLUE CHIP

(Ambi $15) This chunky little yellow car has a red squeaker on the roof and a smiley face with eyes that move as it's pushed along the floor. Scaled just right for small, chubby hands. (310) 645-9680.

■ Earlyears Floor Roller

(International Playthings $14.95) Two see-through rings are loaded with bright beads that tumble and clatter as this unusual floor toy wobbles and rolls with a funny groaning noise. Motivates beginning crawlers to "go for it" and invites exploration once it's in hand. Fun for back-and-forth games of "Roll it to me— I'll roll it to you!" Platinum Award '95. Also, **Magic Chime Ball.** (800) 445-8347.

■ Lego Primo Caterpillar

(Lego Primo $9.99) Press down on the caterpillar's back and it inches forward with a quiet rattle sound. Bumps on the bright green-and-red caterpillar are just right for attaching a yellow-and-black bee or a spotted lady bug. A jolly floor toy for crawlers. 6 mos. & up. Platinum Award '98. (800) 233-8756.

■ Peek-a-Boo Activity Tunnel

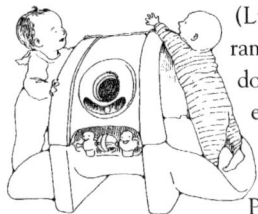

(Little Tikes $45) The gentle up-and-down ramp of this red tunnel with peekaboo window is safe for crawling babies. Our testers enjoyed going round and round again and having a covered hiding place to sit and play with the built-in chunky spinners. Platinum Award '96. (800) 321-0183.

■ Roll-a-Round School Bus

(Fisher-Price $6.99) It's fun to fill this little school bus with two little rolling face balls. Open the back door ramp, and down they roll!

A bright yellow school bus with red wheels has a permanent driver whose face rolls as it's pushed along. Good for crawling and sitting-up babies. 6 mos. & up. (800) 43-KIDS.

■ **Twinky Ball** 🌟

(Gund $7–$12) A patterned black-and-white ball with a band of red, done in soft velour, that jingles and is easy to grasp, toss, and roll. A perfect toy for crawlers to chase and for early back-and-forth roly-poly social games. Also top-rated: BLUE CHIP **Colorfun Ball** ($7–$12), done in primary colors, and a new line of velour sports-themed balls. (732) 248-1500.

> **SAFETY TIP:** While at first glance foam balls may seem like a safe bet, they are not for infants, as small pieces may be chewed off and ingested. This is also true of Nerf-type balls that have a plastic cover that can be chewed through.

> **ACTIVITY TIP:** Where's the ball? As well as rolling the ball back and forth to baby, try this hide-and-seek game: Cover most of the ball with cloth and ask, "Where's the ball?" If your baby doesn't uncover the ball, lift the cover and hide it again. Eventually you can cover the object completely. This game helps baby learn that even if an object can't be seen, it still exists.

First Tub Toys

> **Comparison Shopper—Boat Toys**
> Our testers enjoyed both the **Stack'n'Build Blocks & Boat** (Fisher-Price $7.99) which comes with a sailor and chunky stacking blocks that can be added to the top of the blue boat, and **Tugboat Tubbies** 🌟 (Little Tikes $7.99), which comes with two figures, a boat, and three floating shapes. 6 mos. & up. Fisher-Price (800) 432-5437 / Little Tikes (800) 321-0183.

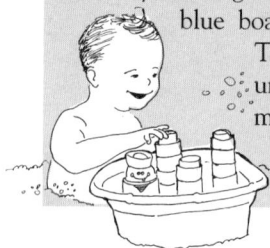

■ **Duck Family**

(Ambi $18) Three little primary-colored plastic ducks and their parent (we make no gender assumptions). Great fun for the bath. The babies store in big duck's body. (310) 645-9680.

SAFETY TIP: The Consumer Product Safety Commission reports 11 deaths and 17 injuries associated with baby bath "supporting rings," devices that keep baby seated in the bath tub. Never rely on such devices to keep baby safe. Going to answer the door or phone can result in serious injury, or worse, to babies and toddlers.

First Huggables

Babies often receive tons of soft dolls that are too big, too fuzzy, and even unsafe for now. Although they may be decorative and fine for gazing at, fuzzy plush dolls with ribbons, buttons, plastic features that may pull out, or doodads that may be pulled off are better saved for preschool years.

When shopping for huggables, look for:

- **Interesting textures**
- **Easy-to-grasp legs or arms**
- **Sound effects sewn safely inside**
- **Washable fabric such as velour or terry cloth**
- **Stitched-on features; no loose ribbons or bells**
- **Small enough size for infant to hold with ease**

■ **Deecha Dolls**

(Manhattan Toy $10 & up) Inspired by young children's drawings of people, these soft velour dolls with totally stitched features are all face and easy-to-grab arms and legs. Will be a hit with the next age group, too. (800) 747-2454.

■ **Lamaze Cuddle Baby**

(Learning Curve $5-$9) Talk about touchy-feely textures—this velour doll with safe stitched features has satin ribbon hat and edging

on her skirt that reverses to black & white checks. Her arms end in little knots for chewing. Also see: other **Little Knotties** dolls that are easy to grasp. New for '99, **Lumps the Camel, Gino the Giraffe** and **Bumbles the Bee.** (800) 704-8697.

■ **My Very Soft Baby**

(Playskool $9.99) An ideal first doll with pliable vinyl face and totally soft, washable pink terry cloth body. Makes pleasant giggly sound when squeezed. African-American version available. (800) 752-9755.

■ **Sleepyhead Bunny** 💥

(North American Bear $12 & $23) These are totally huggable, soft and floppy bunnies in pink or blue striped PJs. Choose either 15" or 8" rattle. The award-winning line of **Velveteenie Circus Animals** ($8–$31), done in vibrant hot colors on soft velour fabric, are still a great choice for this age group and the next. Platinum Award '94. (800) 682-3427.

■ **Touch'n'Crawl Baby Mickey**

(Mattel $20) Choose either Mickey, Goofy, or Donald. While not as touch-sensitive as they look on TV, crawlers enjoyed making them move—even if they had to really give them a shove. Three AA batteries required. 6–24 mos. (800) 524-8697.

■ **Rainbow Rascals Mini Gator & Hippo** 💥

(Eden $8 each) Dressed in hot colors with bright patterns these small 8" soft terrycloth dolls have stitched safe features and fit easily in the hand. 8 months & up. (800) 443-4275.

Best Travel Toys for Infants

Having a supply of several small toys can help divert and entertain small travelers whether you're going out for a day or away for a week. Select several very different toys, for example:

• **Teether**
• **Hand-held mirror**

- **Highchair toy**
- **Small huggable**
- **Familiar quilt to rest on**
- **Musical toy**
- **Books and pictures to share**

■ **3 in 1 Triangle Toy** 🌟

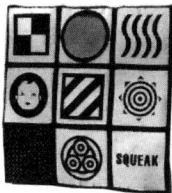

(Wimmer-Ferguson $20) A versatile toy with 18 high-contrast graphic patterns to hang in the car for gazing at. Thanks to magnets inside, can be hung on the fridge or folded into a long wedge for floor play. There's a small mirror, and touchie feelies, as well as a squeaker that will interest older babies. Still highly recommended, the **Car Seat Gallery,** a Blue Chip choice ($12) for back-facing car seats. Hang the 4-way pattern pocket chart on the back seat of the car. Platinum Award '95. (800) 747-2454.

■ **Baby's First Links** 🌟

(Tyco $7.99) Unlike typical links, these are longer, wider, and softer than most, and shaped like Sesame Street characters. A set of eight comes with a star that plays electronic music. Soft enough to gum, these are handy for hanging toys on the car seat or stroller. Birth–2. (800) 488-8697.

> **SAFETY NOTE: Links should never be made into a loop, or linked across a crib or playpen. We often see babies dangerously draped and wrapped in long lengths of links. Warning labels say that a chain of links should never be more than 12" long and should be used with adult supervision.**

🛍 Comparison Shopper— Travel Playmats

Discover and Go Playmat (Wimmer-Ferguson $45) You can fold this playmat into a pouch and hang it on the back of a car seat as a gazing toy for young babies. Open it and use it on the floor as a versatile play environment at home or away. There are peek-a-boo activities, a mirror, squeaker, and teether rattle for all sorts of sensory feedback. Reverses to nonpatterned soft side. (800) 747-2454. In the mass market, you can't go wrong with either the circular **Activity-Go-Round-Quilt** (Little Tikes $20) or the larger-than-usual **Big'n' Bright Quilt** (Playskool $25). Both are soft and washable, and have lots of textured activities for babies to explore. Little Tikes (800) 321-0183 / Playskool (800) 752-9755.

Toddlers-in-Training Toys

Some of the early walking toys found in the next chapter may be ideal for infants who are seriously working on walking before their first birthday.

Best New Baby/Shower Gifts

Big Ticket ($40–50)	**Deluxe Gymini 3-D Activity Gym** (Tiny Love) or **Sensational Circus Musical Mobile** (Manhattan Baby)
Under $40	**Slumbertime Soother** (Fisher-Price) or **Flatso Farm Musical Pulldown** (North American Bear)
Under $30	**Crib Center** (Little Tikes) or **Inchworm Pull Musical** (Manhattan Baby)
Under $20	**Lamaze Peek-a-Boo Puppet** (Learning Curve) or **Puzzle Cube** (Wimmer-Ferguson) or **Baby Laptop** (Little Tikes)
Under $15	**Earlyears Earl E. Bird** (International Playthings) or **Twinky Ball** (Gund) or **3-in-1 Travel Toy** (Wimmer-Ferguson)

Under $10   **Fascination Station** (Sassy) or **Dunk & Clunk Circus Rings** (Sassy) or **Lego Primo Caterpillar** (Lego) or **Flip'n'Play Mirror** (Fisher-Price)

Under $5   **Tolo Deluxe Rattle** (Small World) or **Snap-Lock Beads** (Fisher-Price) or **Shake'n'Roll Surprise Ball** (Lego)

Looking Ahead:
Best First Birthday Gifts For Every Budget

Big Ticket ($50 or more)   **Push Cart** (Galt) or **Dot the Dog** (Hoopla by Andre)

Under $50   **Doors & Drawers Activity Kitchen** (Little Tikes)

Under $30   **Activity Table** (Fisher-Price)

Under $25   **Earlyears Activity Center** (International Playthings)

Under $15   **Bigger Family Van** (Step 2)

Under $10   **Corn Popper** (Fisher-Price)

Under $5   Cardboard book (see Books section)

2 • Toddlers
One to Two Years

What to Expect Developmentally

Active Exploration. Anyone who spends time with toddlers knows that they are active, on-the-go learners. They don't visit long because there are so many places and things to explore. Toys that invite active investigation are best for this age group. For toddlers, toys with doors to open, knobs to push, and pieces to fit, fill, and dump provide the raw material for developing fine motor skills, language, and imagination.

Big-Muscle Play. Toddlers also need playthings that match their newfound mobility and their budding sense of independence. Wheeled toys to push, ride on, and even ride in are great favorites. So is equipment they can climb, rock, and slide on. In these two busy years, toddlers grow from wobbly walkers to nimble runners and climbers.

Language and Pretend Power. As language develops, so does the ability to pretend. For beginners, games of make-believe depend more on action than story lines. Choose props that look like the things they see in the real world.

Toys and Development. Some of the toys in this chapter, such as those for beginning walkers, will have short-term use. However, many of the best products are what we call bridge toys, playthings that will be used now and for several years ahead. While no toddler needs all the toys listed here, one- and two-year-olds do need a good mix of toys that fit varying play modes—toys for indoors and out, for quiet, solo sit-down times, and social run-and-shout-out-loud times. A rich variety of playthings (which may include a plain paper shopping bag or some pots and pans) gives kids the learning tools they need to stretch their physical, intellectual, and social development.

Your Role in Play. Playing (and keeping up) with an active toddler requires a sense of humor and realistic expectations. In order to satisfy their growing appetite for independence, select uncomplicated toys that won't frustrate their sense of "can do" power. For example, if your toddler does not want to sit down with you and work on a puzzle now, she may be willing in an hour, or she may be telling you that it's too difficult and should be put away and tried again in a few weeks.

A Word on Sharing. It's premature to expect a toddler to share. While you can introduce the concept, do not be cha-grined if your toddler screams, "It's mine!" Reassuring a toddler that she will get her toy back or perhaps reminding her that her friend shares his toys when you visit are gentle ways of teaching a very difficult con-cept that will be much easier as she reaches the next stage.

BASIC GEAR CHECKLIST FOR ONES

✓ Push toys	✓ Pull toys
✓ Ride-on toy	✓ Small vehicles
✓ Musical toys	✓ Huggables
✓ Toy phone	✓ Lightweight ball
✓ Fill-and-dump toys	
✓ Manipulatives with moving parts	

BASIC GEAR CHECKLIST OR TWOS

✓Ride-on/-in toy   ✓Push toy
✓Big lightweight ball   ✓Shovel and pail
✓Climbing/sliding toy   ✓Art supplies
✓Big blocks   ✓Table and chair
✓Huggables   ✓Props for housekeeping
✓Simple puzzles/shape-sorters

Toys to Avoid

These toys pose choking and/or suffocation hazards:

✓Foam toys
✓Toys with small parts (including small plastic fake foods)
✓Dolls and stuffed animals with fuzzy and/or long hair
✓Toys labeled 3 & up (no matter how smart toddlers are! The label almost always indicates that there are small parts in or on the toy)
✓Latex balloons (Note: The Consumer Product Safety Commission reports that latex balloons are the leading cause of suffocation deaths! Since 1973 more than 110 children have died from suffocation involving uninflated balloons or pieces of broken ones. They are not advised for children under age six.)

These toys are developmentally inappropriate:

✓Electronic educational drill toys
✓Shape-sorters with more than three shapes
✓Battery-operated ride-ons
✓Pedal toys

Active Physical Play

Beginning walkers will get miles of use from a low-to-the-ground, stable wheeled toy. The products on the market are not created equal. Here are some basic things to look for:

- The wobbly toddler may use the toy to pull up on, so you'll want to find one that is weighted and won't tip easily.

- Try before you buy. Some ride-ons are scaled for tall kids, others for small kids.

- Toddlers do not need battery-powered ride-ons! Encourage foot power, not push-button action!

- Toddlers are not ready for pedals. Four wheels and two feet on the ground are best.

- Toys with loud and constant sound effects may be appealing in the store, but can become annoying in tight spaces.

For Younger Toddlers:
■ Grow'n'Go Walker Mower

(Tyco $24.99) Our newly walking tester loved pushing this sturdy plastic mower that makes a poppity noise when pushed. Elmo, on the top of the mower, also bobs up and down as it goes. Well-balanced for new walkers. (800) 488-8697.

■ Push Cart

(Galt $79.95) This recently re-styled classic wooden cart is pricier than any of its plastic counterparts but can be passed down to younger siblings! Very stable for early walkers and a perfect first wagon for carting treasures. (800) 899-4258.

Wagons, Prams, & Ride-ons for Steady-on-their-Feet Toddlers
■ Baby Walker

(Lego Primo $25) Lego's bright plastic pushing wagon is not weighted and is designed for steady walkers. Designed for young toddlers for moving about with cargo. 1 & up. A **Lego Primo Elephant** ride-on looked promising but was not ready for testing.(800) 233-8756.

■ Bigger Family Construction Wagon

(Step 2 $19.99) Bright yellow wagon with a flat cargo bed is ideal for carting about blocks and other favorite treasures. Four chunky wheels make a clicking sound when pushed or pulled with sturdy blue handle.

Comes with two Bigger Family people. They say 1 & up; best suited for steady walkers. Also top-rated: **Walk Me Wagon** ($20); **Push About Fire Truck** (Step 2 $23) comes with a pull or push handle for pulling or pushing this big truck that's scaled for early pretend play. Platinum Award '98. (800) 347-8372.

■ Little People Push'n'Pull Fire Truck

(Fisher-Price $14.99) For push and pull action toddlers use the ladder/handle that swivels and folds down for dramatic play. Has a bell and firefighter with a Dalmatian fire dog. Looked promising but was not ready for testing. 1 1/2–4. (800) 432-5437.

■ Doll's Prams

(Little Tikes $24 & Brio $55) Brio's gender-free wooden pram is not a walker for beginners—it tips. It's for steady-on-their-feet true walkers. For a more gender-specific and less pricey version, see Little Tikes classic plastic buggy. Either are fine for beginning pretend. 2s & up. Little Tikes (800) 321-0183 / Brio (888) 274-6869.

First Ride-Ons

■ Dot the Dog

(Manhattan Toy $60) For tots who are steady on their feet, a rocking toy is fun. Save the big wooden and plastic kinds for later. This low-to-the-ground soft fabric dog has a gentle action with jingle sounds. 1 & up. (800) 541-1345.

■ Push & Ride Racer & Semi Truck

(Little Tikes $20) The latest ride-on entries from this company and others do not measure up to earlier versions. Neither the new **Push & Ride Racer** nor the **Push & Ride Semi Truck** have true steering ability and both are harder for new walkers to get on easily—especially if they have short legs. That said, these are now the best choices, but have your child test-drive either for size. 1–3. (800) 321-0183.

■ **Load & Ride Dump Truck**

(Little Tikes $35) Junior construction workers will be able to move mountains as they straddle and ride this pedal-less truck for loading and dumping fun. The dump has a low lip to keep cargo from sliding out. 1 1/2–4. (800) 321-0183.

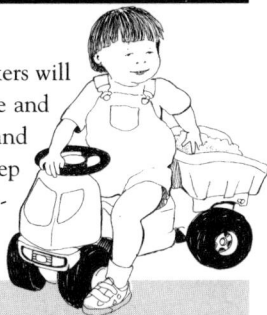

🛍 **Comparison Shopper— Plastic Cars**

You can't go wrong with either the **Super Car** (Today's Kids $40) or the **Cozy Coupe Car** (Little Tikes $40). Our testers found them to be a toss-up. Both are brightly colored and have no licensed characters to make them trendy or gender-specific. Both built to last! An ideal choice for pretend and physical play. 2 & up. Little Tikes (800) 321-0183 / Today's Kids (800) 258-8697. See Preschool Chapter for more choices.

Push and Pull Toys

Push comes before pull. Instead of holding on to someone's hand, young toddlers often find sheer joy in the independence of walking while holding on to a push toy. You may even have had Fisher-Price's BLUE CHIP **Corn Popper** *($8) or* **Chime Roller** *($8) which are still great choices. (800) 432-5437. Some of the best of these toys will also be used for pretend play. Pull toys are for older tots who are surefooted and can look over a shoulder without tripping.*

■ **Miss Spider** 🏆 **PLATINUM AWARD**

(Learning Curve $34.99) This bright yellow wooden spider would not frighten Miss Muffet or any toddler. Borrowed from the Miss Spider series of books for older kids, she spins her many legs as she's pulled along. Fun! Also top-rated, friendly, colorful and ratchety **Finnegan the Dragon** ($34.99). 18 mos. & up. (800) 704-8697.

> **SAFETY TIP: Avoid pull toys with springs and beads that many toddlers will try to eat. Old pull toys from the attic may have dangerous levels of lead paint.**

■ Spinning Bus

(Battat $15) Eight little animal and people passengers plus a driver spin as this pull toy rolls along. There's a ramp for taking passengers off and on. Fun for games of loading, unloading, and rearranging the multiple pieces as well as refining dexterity to fit them on their posts. 8 mos. & up. (800) 247-6144.

NOTABLE PREVIOUS WINNERS:

Kouvalias' BLUE CHIP jaunty green wooden **Little Cricket Pull Toy** ($40). This line of toys is pricey but can be passed along. 2 & up. (800) 445-8347. For a less pricey plastic pull toy, **Max** (Ambi $25), is an adorable black-and-white pooch. 1 1/2 & up. (310) 645-9680; or Fisher-Price's classic **Little Snoopy** ($8) that wags his tail as he walks. (800) 432-KIDS.

> **FREEBIE: Your toddler's favorite toy may be a big shopping bag to fill, dump, and tote around. Empty plastic soda bottles with lids and rings removed make big but lightweight cargo.**

Balls

Big, lightweight balls for tossing, kicking, chasing, or social back-and-forth, roly-poly games are favorite pieces of basic gear. Soft fabric balls or slightly deflated beach balls are the best choice for now. Avoid foam and balloon-filled balls that are a choking hazard if nibbled.

■ Toddler Golf

(Playskool $17.99) Our tester liked the fill-and-spill action of this special golf set. You drop the balls in the hopper and they roll out onto the "green" one at a time. Comes with a fat golf club that fits tots to a tee! 2 & up. (800) PLAYSKL.

Strictly Outdoors:
Climbers, Wading Pools, Sandboxes, Props for the Sandbox, Gardening Tools, Top-Rated Lawn Mower, and Snow Fun

First Climbers
Climbers are great for big-muscle play for toddlers who are steady on their feet. There are more climbers in the preschool chapter; these are designed for both toddlers and young preschoolers to enjoy.

■**Junior Activity Gym** BLUE CHIP

(Little Tikes $70) This pint-sized version of Little Tikes' classic Activity Gym is low to the ground, and will be used as a climber, roof-free play house, and slide. It has no steps, so toddlers must pull themselves up in order to use the slide. 1 1/2 & up. (800) 321-0183.

■ **8-in-1 Adjustable Playground**

(Little Tikes $280) A combo playhouse, tunnel, climber, and double slide that the whole gang can play on together. Done in hot colors, this big piece of equipment provides for physical and dramatic play. Parent testers hated the picture of a smiling man on the instructions, but admitted that their 2- & 4-year-olds really enjoyed the playground. Hard to assemble. 2 & up. (800) 321-0183.

Wading Pools
Our testers preferred inexpensive hard-vinyl wading pools to those that had to be blown up or filled with water to hold a shape (most of these had sides that were too high for younger toddlers to climb over by themselves). Prefab wading pools are also easier to lift, dump and clean. You'll find an adequate no-frills pool for under $20.

Sandboxes

While small boxes are good choices when space is a concern, keep in mind that a bigger box will give more than one child enough room to maneuver. We looked for smooth edges and strong sides that will support a child's weight. The motif is really a personal preference. You can't go wrong with any of the following—all come with covers. Unless you can't spare the space, this is a case where more is more. Small boxes will be outgrown quickly.

Our favorites: On the small side, **Frog Sandbox** (Step 2 $35) or **Green Turtle** (Little Tikes $40). 1 & up. Bigger choices: **Crabbie Sandbox** (Step 2 $45) or **Dinosaur Sandbox** (Little Tikes $55). Bigger still: **Tuggy II Sandbox & Splasher** (Step 2 $60) There's plenty of room for several kids to play together and built-in pretend power with a captain's wheel for steering the jolly boat anywhere! Can be used as pool instead. 2 & up. Step 2 (800) 347-8372 / Little Tikes (800) 321-0183.

Sandbox Props: A basic bucket from any toy store will do—just be sure to check for smooth edges.

FREEBIE: Many of the best props for the sandbox are in your kitchen: a plastic colander, an empty margarine container, strainers, squeeze bottles, etc.

Water Sprinklers

Many sprinklers are too overwhelming for toddlers and some preschoolers. We suggest low-to-the-ground ones with gentle action. Here are two good choices for getting their feet wet, so to speak.

■ Elmo's 1-2-3 Sprinkler

(Tyco $14.99) Elmo has three different settings, the first being just a gentle spray. (800) 488-8697.

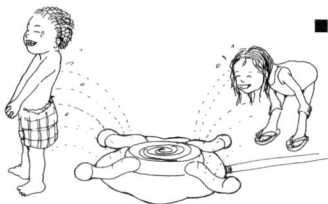

■ **Waterpark Whirlee Sprinkler**
(Little Tikes $15) Low-to-the-ground and gentle. (800) 321-0183. For other sprinklers, see Preschool Chapter.

FREEBIE: Painting with water is a neat outdoors activity for older toddlers. A paintbrush and bucket of water produce satisfying but temporary effects—early lessons in evaporation or magic: take your pick!

The Youngest Gardener
see Preschool Chapter

Snow Fun

■ **Deluxe Toddler Sleigh**
BLUE CHIP

(Flexible Flyer $30) Ready for dashing through the snow, this bright-red toddler sled has high, sloping sides, molded side runners, safety seat belt, and strong yellow towrope. A great winter get-about. Toy Supermarkets.

SHOPPING TIP: A child-sized snow shovel can provide great pretend and active play. Any toy supermarket will have one. Just be on the lookout for sharp edges.

Sit-Down Play

First Puzzles and Manipulatives

Toddlers enjoy toys that invite investigation but don't demand too much dexterity. Toys with lids to lift, buttons to push, and dials to turn give them satisfying feedback along with playful ways to devel-

op fine motor skills and eye/hand coordination.
Many of these are for older toddlers with greater dexterity.

First Puzzles

For toddlers, stick with the whole-piece puzzles. We were disappointed again this
year to find poorly crafted wooden puzzles with splinters. Our best advice is to
check before you buy, or stick to cardboard or vinyl. Top-Rated
Sets: **Kid Smart Puzzles** (Learning Curve $7–$11) (800)
704-8697; **My First Puzzles** (Playskool's $5) 2 & up,
(800) 752-9755; **Picturebook
art** (Mudpuppy $8.95) 2 & up,
(212) 354-8840; and **Familiar
Things** (Lauri $18.95) Twelve 2-piece
vinyl puzzles of familiar objects (pictured
left). 2 & up, (800) 451-0520.

Manipulatives

■ Early Start Activity Center

(International Playthings $19.95) With just a touch, the
rolling beads, clacking shapes, and rattling balls all
respond to toddler's investigations. Sound, color, and
action make this an appealing toy for eye/hand skills
and learning about cause and effect. 1 & up.
Platinum Award '96. (800) 445-8347.

■ Activity Table ⭐ PLATINUM AWARD

(Fisher-Price $29.99) The best activity table for tod-
dlers we've seen in years. Can be used by babies
on the floor and for standing at by tots. Table
top flips from a surface for stacking with
Stack'n'Build blocks to an activity center with
whirling marbles (safely enclosed), mirror, peek-
a-boo flippers, and chute for filling and spilling the
blocks. 9 mos. & up. (800) 432-5437.

■ Ball Party Roll Around Tower

(International Playthings/Tomy $24.99) Hands down, one of the best
toys for this age group. Toddlers love the repetitive action of making
the balls roll down the tower. Be prepared—this is noisy but great

fun. **Pick Up Tube** ($9.99) actually makes picking up ten colorful balls into a game. They say 1 & up, we'd say save these for 18–36 months. Platinum Award '98. (800) 445-8347.

■ Beads on Wire Toys BLUE CHIP

(Anatex and Educo $15 & up) Both of these companies make wonderful tracking toys with tethered down colored beads of different shapes and sizes that can be moved up, down, and around curved and twisted wire mazes. These abstract toys develop eye/hand skills, language, counting, and pretending. 1 1/2 & up. Anatex (800) 999-9599 / Educo (800) 661-4142.

Comparison Shopper — Hammer Toys

Up & Down Hammer Bench (Learning Curve $24.99) looks like a traditional wooden version but with an added twist for safety—as one peg is hit, another one pops up—none come out. (800) 704-8697. **Earlyears Pound'n'Play** (International Playthings $13) plastic version with four colorful balls. (800) 445-8347. Also very special for **Pound A Ball** (Battat $18), a three-level tower as shown here with a see-through window. 1 1/2 & up. (800) 247-6144.

■ Spinning Balls Top

(Battat $17) Push the red hat on the bear's head and the colorful balls and spiral graphic spin inside the see-through dome. For extra visual interest there's a shiny reflective tube and clattering sound as the balls spin. Push fast enough and the balls almost disappear! 1 & up. Also top-rated: **Mini Spinning Top** ($15) with marble sized balls. (800) 247-6144.

■ Teddy Bear Carousel

(Ambi $26) Push down on the big yellow knob and the yellow and red teddy bears inside the dome will spin quietly. A flat-bottomed top that's easy enough for toddlers to learn to activate with independence. 1 1/2 & up.

(310) 645-9680.

First Construction Toys

For the youngest toddlers, filling, dumping, and knocking down blocks comes before lining them up or stacking. Start with **Lego Primo** and Fisher Price's **Stacking Blocks** (see infant chapter). Twos and up will start enjoying big cardboard blocks with adults who are willing to get down on the floor and make long roadways, towers, and bridges. Older twos will enjoy plastic blocks, such as **Duplo** and **Mega Blocks**.

■ Lego Primo

(Lego Systems $4–$25) Day after day, toddler testers returned to these colorful stacking blocks with soft edges and rounded bumps that make for an easy fit—even by little hands. Designed to stimulate the senses, some have rattle sounds, a mirror, chubby people and animal figures, a wheeled car base, and even a rock-and-spin block that twirls like a top. 6–24 mos. Platinum Award '96. (800) 233-8756.

> **SAFETY TIP: Baby blocks are being marketed this year in large plastic bags. While they have warnings on them to meet regulations and they do make convenient storage containers, throw them away at once! Large plastic bags are dangerous around babies and toddlers. An open basket is a safer choice.**

■ Giant Constructive Blocks BLUE CHIP

(Constructive Playthings $15.95) These sturdy 12" x 6" x 4" cardboard blocks are printed like red bricks and great for stacking into towers, walls, and other big but lightweight creations. Strong enough to stand on, these classic blocks endure years of creative use. Set of 12. #CP-626. (800) 832-0572.

■ Duplo School Bus PLATINUM AWARD

(Lego $29.99) A wow-wee kind of gift. Older toddlers can ride on top of this yellow school bus, come to a stop, and use the roof as a base

for their Duplo creations. Comes with 70 pieces and room for lots
more. A great value. 2 & up. (800) 233-8756.

■ Mega Blocks Wagon

(Mega Blocks $30) A tot-sized red wagon loaded with 75 pieces of
oversized plastic pegged blocks will be fun for making big, fast constructions. Pegs on side of wagon can be used for building up and
over. 2 years & up. (800) 465-6342.

First Nesting, Stacking, and Shape-Sorter Toys:
Ring & Post Toys 🏅

*Classic stackers are usually lost before tots are develop-
mentally able to put them in size order. Here are better choices for beginners because there's no right or
wrong way:* **Circus Rings** *(Sassy $6.99) Interesting
patterns, colors, and textures make the one-size stacking rings fool-proof for tots to teethe, toss, or stack.
(800) 323-6336.*

　　Rock'n'Stack *(Lego Primo $8.99)
Five size-order pieces stack with a cheerful
red bear head on the top. Unlike old stacking toys
with posts, this "post-less" one works even if the pieces
are not put in size order, so there's no rigid
right or wrong way. 1 & up. (800) 233-
8756.*

Nesting and Stacking Toys 🏅

*Toddlers like the multiple pieces for banging and stacking
long before they can nest them. In fact,
they'll knock them down before they can
fit them together. Eventually, stacking
and nesting toys develop hand/eye coordination, size-order concepts, and counting. Here
are some good choices:* **Stacking Cups** *(Sassy
$5.50) There are four interesting textures on
the rims of these boldly patterned cups for
young toddlers. 1 & up. (800) 323-
6336.* **Sort and Stack Set** *(Battat
$13) 10-piece set with shapes, large nesting cups, and
a shape-sorter. (800) 247-6144.* **Nesting Boxes** *(Ambi $12.95)*

Six plastic boxes with lids for matching. 2 & up. (310) 645-9680.

Tot Tower ✸ (eeboo $18) Handsome cardboard nesting blocks with familiar objects to know and name. The newest version has multi-ethnic toddlers' faces and a range of feelings in their expression. 1 & up. (212) 222-0823.

■ Count and Match Pegboard BLUE CHIP

(Battat $12) Little hands will be busy with the 25 easy-to-grasp, brightly colored chunky pegs that can be sorted by color or shape on the 10"-square base. Pegs can be stacked and eventually strung like beads. 2 & up. (800) 247-6144.

■ Matchin' Keys Pet Shop ✸

(Fisher-Price $14.99) You know how much toddlers love keys, but most toys with doors and keys are just too hard. Surprise! This one really works! Color-coded keys open pop-open doors. Develops visual skills, dexterity and sense of can-do. Testers loved fitting the pets on their peg-seats. 2 & up. (800) 432-5437.

■ Little Smart Sort 'n Go Car ✸

(Vtech $14.99) A jaunty yellow vehicle has musical shape-sorter windows that play as each shape is placed inside the car. They all empty out of the trunk. We applaud the volume control on this toy, which also can be used as a pull toy. (800) 420-8100. 2 1/2 & up.

Pretend Play

As language develops, older toddlers begin their early games of pretend. So much of the real equipment tots see adults using is off-limits to them. Child-sized versions can (sometimes) offer a satisfying alternative and fuel the imagination of little ones who love to mimic what they see you doing. Never again will sweeping and cleaning be more fun than to a toddler!

Dolls and Huggables

Both boys and girls enjoy playing with dolls and soft animals. For one year olds, velour and short-haired plush animals will now hold some interest. Huggables classics such as **Snuffles** or **Winnie the Pooh** (Gund) and **Spot** (Eden) may become long-loved companions for play and naptime. Older toddlers like oversized but lightweight huggables such as **Raggedy Ann & Andy** (Applause) to love and lug about. Bald baby dolls to take in the tub and classics like **Cabbage Patch Kids** (Mattel) with yarn hair and soft bodies are available in boy, girl, and multi-ethnic versions. Toddlers also like smaller take-along dolls that fit in their fists. Since toddlers are still likely to chew on their toys, select uncomplicated huggables without small decorations, long hair, or accessories that can be pulled off.

SAFETY TIP: Do not leave large plush dolls or toys in crib as they can be stepped on and accidentally give tots a boost over the side.

■ Babi Corolle

(Corolle $13 & up) When you're looking for a toddler's first baby doll you probably won't find a better choice than these soft huggable babies that feel big but light. Totally washable, **Pierrot** ($20), a clown with knitted face and parachute nylon body, is a bright and happy armful. Or, consider the sweet, fabric-faced **First Mates** ($30), a big 10" doll with 5" baby in red, white, and blue knits. 1 & up. (800) 628-3655.

■ Flax or Rye Bear

(Manhattan Toy $15 each) Super soft and washable 16" teddies are totally right for toddlers to lug and love. Easy to grab with long floppy legs and arms and stitched features, and trimmed with twill bows with a homemade look and feel. Also, **Corduroys** ($15) 8" bear is wonderfully textured. 1 & up. For older tots, **Gigi Giraffe** ($20) is a 20" huggable with stitched features, yarn mane, and long floppy legs and neck. 2 & up. (800) 541-1345.

■ Flatolamb, Flatocow, Flatopig & Flatoduck 🎀

(North American Bear Co. $10 & up) Take your
pick of any of these soft velour farmyard
critters—a cow, lamb, pig, or duck.
Also available as huggables (15")
or rattles (9"). Big 25" versions
are light but big enough to satisfy a tot's
love for big, big, big. (800) 682-3427.

■ Groovy Girls
🎀 PLATINUM AWARD

(Manhattan Toy $10 each) Soft, adorable,
floppy, long-legged velour dolls with
stitched features, yarn hair and groovy
flower-power '60s clothes. A perfect
fistful for toddlers' pretend play. 2 &
up. (800) 541-1345.

■ Ragtime Dog & Cat

(North American Bear $24 each) A sunny yellow dog and hot pink
cat with embroidered features make cheerful huggable companions.
Made of a non-plush felt-like fabric, they wear floral clothes with
Velcro closures. Machine washable. Also charming, **Baby's First
Critters** ($20 each). 1 & up. (800) 682-3427.

■ Snookums

(Mattel $20) These scented 12" bald baby dolls with beanbag bodies
have removable cotton rompers and opened eyes to avoid a small
parts problem. Available in several skin tones. (800) 524-8697.

**SAFETY TIP: Toddlers should not have pillow-like dolls
or toys to sleep with or dolls with chewable doodads
and features that pose a choking hazard.**

■ Teletubbies 🎀

(Playskool $24) We agree with the critics who say that
the Teletubbies do little to devel-
op children's language, and that
their non-verbal sounds mirror
rather than expand children's
verbal skills. That said, our kid

testers enjoyed hugging the dolls that say a few phrases from the show. 2 & up. (800) 752-9755.

■ Wrinkles 🌟

(Manhattan Toy $60) Little floor sitters will like flopping over a giant 24" golden-colored, short-haired, wrinkly-faced dog. New for '99, a smaller 14" **Wrinkles Jr.** ($20) 2 & up. (800) 541-1345.

■ Yum Yum Cookie Monster
🌟 PLATINUM AWARD

(Tyco $29.99) Hands down, our favorite novelty doll of the year. When his cookie goes into his mouth, Cookie Monster waves his arms and makes Cookie Monster sounds. Very cute! 2 & up. (800) 367-8926.

Doll Accessories

Most toddlers will try to get into doll furniture you buy. Better to wait until the next stage for more elaborate baby beds, highchairs, and strollers. See Preschool section for best bets.

Vehicles

■ Bigger Family Van

(Step 2 $13) Four big play figures—a mom, dad, brother, and sister—are fun to load and unload in the big family van that's scaled for toddlers' roll-about games. Also in the same line, the **Bigger Family School Bus.** 1 & up. Platinum Award '98. (800) 347-8372.

■ Elmo and His Pet Puppy 🌟 PLATINUM AWARD

(Tyco $29.99) Our 2 1/2-year-old tester's face lit up with a smile when he squeezed Elmo's hands and made the little radio-controlled puppy walk and spin. This novelty toy is for older toddlers and preschoolers, too. We still love **Elmo's Radio Control Stunt Plane** ($20), with a single button control that makes Elmo's plane twirl and swings Elmo out of the cockpit. It's super easy to operate.

Platinum Award '98. New but not as easy to operate, **Elmo's Bump 'n'Go RC.** All take 2 AA and 1 9V batteries. 2 1/2. (800) 488-8697.

■ Loader & Dump Truck

(Little Tikes $12 each) Like this company's big classic plastic construction vehicles, these are working trucks for the sandbox, but slightly scaled down in size and price. Lightweight enough to take along to the beach or park they have working parts that really lift and spill. A great birthday gift for 2s & up. (800) 321-0183.

School Buses ★99★

We are delighted that both Fisher-Price's **Little People School Bus** *($14.99) and Little Tikes'* **School Toddle Tots School Bus** *($12.99) come with rear ramps, wheelchairs and play people. Passengers can also be loaded in toddler fashion through the open roof. You can't go wrong with either. 1 1/2–5. Fisher-Price (800) 432-5437 / Little Tikes (800) 321-0183.*

■ Stack'n'Build Choo Choo ★99★

(Fisher-Price $14.99) Fits together easily with the rounded stacking blocks. The 10-piece set has a red engine, two cars, and plenty of other rounded blocks and characters that link the train together. Says 6–36 months. We'd say tots 12–24 months are the right target age. (800) 432-5437.

■ Roadworks

(Ambi $20 each) Three super-duper plastic trucks in bright colors are just right for toddlers. There's a van with drop tailgate for cargo, a jaunty tipper truck that tips, and a working tow truck. 1 & up. Platinum Award '97. (310) 645-9680.

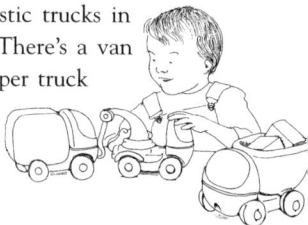

Housekeeping Props

Older toddlers, both boys and girls, adore imitating the real work they see grown-ups doing around the house. Sweeping the floor, vacuuming, cooking, caring for the baby—these are thrilling roles to play. Many of

the props for this sort of pretend will be used for several years. They are what we call "bridge toys" that span the years.

■ Push'n'Puff Vac

(Fisher-Price $16.99) Just like the real thing, this innovative vacuum cleaner has a fabric bag that expands as it's pushed. Makes a somewhat noisy sound as it rolls. Fun for sure footed walkers and for long term pretend play. 2–6. Platinum Award '98. (800) 432-5437.

> **SAFETY TIP: Buckets!** Beware of buckets used in the house for cleaning. Ever-curious toddlers have been known to fall into them and drown. Old buckets from building bricks also pose a problem. Most new play buckets have a new safety bar halfway down to prevent tots from putting their head all the way in.

■ Whirlin' Vac

(Playskool $12.99) This looks just like your hand-held vac but it has a see-through window where dust balls whirl and a humming motor sound when pressed down and rolled. Comes loaded with 2 C batteries. Says 1 & up; we'd say more like old 2s. (800) 752-9755.

Phones

Before you buy a play phone with sound, put the receiver to your ear. Many were alarmingly loud. The quietest of the bunch is Ambi's **City Phone** *($12) that has a spinning face, a mirror, a good clicking sound, and lots of buttons to push. Also quiet,* **Pocket Phone** *(Chicco $10). (310) 645-9680.*

For more bells and whistles: **Cellular Phone** *(Tomy $6) with a pop-up antenna and flashing lights. 1 & up. (800) 445-8347. Also,* **Sesame Street Softy Sounds Phone** *(Tyco $8.99), which has sound effects, a bell that lights, and a peek-a-boo slide. 1 & up. (800) 488-8697. For a more elaborate phone,* **Follow-the-Lights Talking Phone** *(Mattel $30) will appeal to toddlers, and for preschoolers it even teaches them*

their home number. (800) 524-8697.

> **SAFETY TIP: An old real phone may seem like lots of fun, but the cord and small parts pose a choking hazard to toddlers.**

Toy Dishes and Pots

Finding a sturdy, gender-free set of dishes isn't easy! Many sets we tested cracked, were too small for little hands, and were very, very pink! Stay away from sets with small parts, sharp cutlery, and of course, save the pottery and china for later.

Dishes and Tea Sets:

Little Helper's Dining Room & Pots and Pans (Step 2 $11) White, red, and yellow 22-piece set comes with dishes, pots, and utensils. (800) 347-8372.

Tea Set (Battat $10) done in primary colors with a teapot that really pours (surprisingly, not true of most!) and 4 simple cups and saucers with a sugar bowl and creamer. (800) 247-6144.

Tea Set (T.C. Timber $29.95) A handsome primary colored set with pot for pouring, cups, plates, sugar/creamer, spoon, and tray. Pricey, but microwave and dishwasher safe. (800) 245-7622

Cooking sets:

My Cooking Playset (Battat $25) with 41 pieces in primary colors will appeal to junior chefs. Remove cutlery for kids who still mouth toys. (800) 247-6144.

Pretend & Play Set (Learning Resources $14.99) 10-piece cooking set in primary colors including a frying pan, a pot,

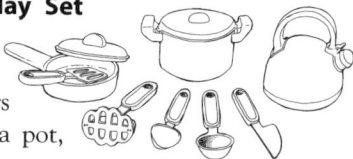

big grip utensils, and our favorite—another tea kettle that actually holds water. 3 & up. (800) 222-3909.

Super Cookware Set ⭐ (Little Tikes $13) 18-piece bake set in Fiesta '40s colors (not quite pink) with a rolling pin, pots, spoons, a cookie cutter, and muffin pan. 2 & up. Still top-rated: **Kitchen Ware.** (800) 321-0183.

SAFETY TIP: Toddlers do not need fake food! Since they mouth most toys, you'll want to avoid small phony food that's especially tempting to "eat" and may be a choking hazard.

Toy Kitchens & Laundries

■ Doors & Drawers Activity Kitchen

(Little Tikes $40) This is a play setting for the youngest chefs. Our toddlers loved playing with this kitchen, which had doors to open, dials to turn, and a telephone for pretend. Platinum Award '97. (800) 321-0183.

■ Townhouse Kitchen ⭐

(Step 2 $65) This combo kitchen with stove, oven, microwave, fridge and phone takes up little space. Also top-rated: **Townhouse Laundry** with washer/dryer, fold-out ironing boards, hanging rack for clothes, and phone. We wish you could get doll's clothes wet here.(800) 347-8372.

■ Country Kitchen ⭐

(Little Tikes $200) The newest in the big line plastic kitchens, complete with coffee maker, double sink, pull-out counter, and coffee-maker! Gender-free colors. For a slightly smaller version, Step 2's **Homestyle Kitchen** has many of the same features. It's really a size and style preference

call. We still like the design of last year's **Family Kitchen** (Little Tikes $75), which is colorful and has a highchair built in. 2 & up. (800) 321-0183.

SHOPPING TIP: If you are looking for a wooden kitchen, you'll need to shop the school catalogs. We found some handsome free-standing appliances in the Constructive Playthings catalog. We liked the sinks with lift-out tub for soap and water play! (800) 832-0572.

Miniature Pretend Settings

■ **Little People House**

(Fisher-Price $29.99) White with red working doors and a blue roof (disregard the lavender on box), this refreshingly non-pink doll house will be enjoyed by boys and girls, and includes a family and chunky furniture that store away. 2 & up. Platinum Award '97. (800) 432-5437. Also, **Little People Farm** (Fisher-Price $30) This fold-and-go farm comes with eight animals and has four stalls with swinging gates. Note: While the hay and pumpkin in this set pass the choke-tube test, they are, in our opinion, still too small and should be removed. 1 1/2 & up. (800) 432-5437.

SAFETY TIP: Fisher-Price Little People made before 1991 pose a choking hazard to children under three. The company has since enlarged the product.

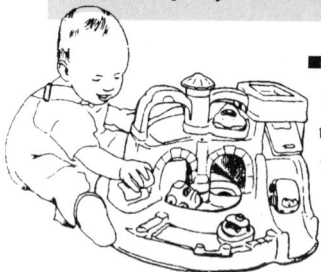

■ **Roll-a-Round Action Town**

(Fisher-Price $24.99) Talk about making things happen! Pull the big red lever and this jolly action toy spins vehicles on two levels in opposite directions. Easy-to-activate with pay-offs that reinforce a child's sense of can-do. Little vehicles have cylinders with changing faces that add to the fun, plus a ramp for cars to roll down and a wavy "sea" to rock the boat. Also notable: **Roll-a-Round School Bus** (800) 432-KIDS.

> **FREEBIE: Empty, staple-free boxes are among the best toys known to toddlers. Great for sitting in, climbing out of, coloring on, lugging around, or loading up.**

Art and Music

Art Supplies

Encourage your toddler to explore colors and textures. This is not the time for coloring books and drawing within the lines. Scribbling comes before drawing, just as crawling comes before walking! You can give your toddler a sense of "can do" power by providing big, easy-to-grasp crayons and blank paper, bright tempera paint with thick brushes, or play-dough and fingerpaints for lively hands-on fun!

You'll need to supervise and establish a place where art materials can be used. If your toddler persists in eating supplies or spreading them on floors or walls, put them away for a while and try again in a month or two.

■ Kid's First Washable Crayons

(Crayola $3) These washable crayons are very big to match toddler's way of grasping with a whole fist. Save the smaller crayons which snap in tots' hands for their school days. If toddler can't resist tasting them, put them away and try again in a few months. 1 1/2 & up. (800) 272-9652.

Making Dough

Playing with pre-made or homemade dough is marvelous for twos who love pounding, poking, rolling, crumbling, and hands-on exploring. At this stage the finished product is unimportant. The focus is on smashing a lump flat or pulling it apart into small pieces or mixing blue and yellow to get green. Dough should be used with supervision in an established place for messy play. Beginners will try to taste: It's non-toxic but not for eating. Put it away if they insist on mouthing and try again in a few weeks.

■ Play-Doh Case of Colors

(Hasbro $7) Imagine a 12-pack with a two-ounce lump of a dozen different colors. Don't let them see all the tubs; open one or two at a time at most. Add plastic dishes for added pretend! 2 & up. (800) 752-9755.

> **FREEBIE: Save money by making your own dough with this homemade play-dough recipe. Kids will enjoy getting their hands into the bowl and helping to mix up dough, which can be stored in a covered container. Mix together 1 cup of flour, 1/3 cup salt, a few drops of vegetable oil and enough water to form a dough. Food coloring or a splash of bright tempera paint can be added.**

Paints and Easels
See Preschool Section

Musical Toys

■ Musical Jack in the Box

(Small World $15) Turn the yellow knob to play "This Old Man" until the Jack in the box pops up with its smile and rosy red nose. May be too surprising for some tots, but most will come to love the predictable and repetitive pop! 1 1/2 & up. (310) 645-9680.

■ Musical Maracas

(Brio $24) Shake and rattle these bright plastic maracas with dial to turn, button to slide, and flute mouthpiece to toot. 2 & up. (888) 274-6869.

■ Rap-a-Tap Rhythm Set BLUE CHIP

(Little Tikes $20) Shake, rattle, and feel the beat. These safe, chunky rhythm instruments are perfect for the youngest music makers. Maracas, in bright orange, have see-through dome so tots can see the balls inside. Purple tambourine is easy to play and makes a pleasant

enough sound. (800) 321-0183.

■ Select-A-Station Stereo

(Playskool $14.99) We are giving fair warning: This is a very loud musical toy. Turn the dial to choose pop, classical, country, or easy listening (sort of). Has a carrying handle, but if you are traveling, we suggest you put this in the trunk. Takes 2 AA batteries. 2 & up. (800) 752-9755.

Bath Toys

> **SAFETY TIP: Foam bath toys are a choking hazard to toddlers, who may bite off pieces. Unfortunately, many of the age labels on such products are in very small print.**

■ Stack 'n Learn Boat ★

(Lego Primo $9.99) When you take this chunky little boat, passenger, and "smokestack" out of the box don't think there's something wrong if it doesn't go "tuut" like the picture on the box. Put it into the tub and let the fun begin. Tap the sailor or the stack in water and they do go "tuut." Scoop water in the stack and it sprinkles, too! 1 & up. (800) 233-8756

■ Lamaze Tub Frogs ★

(Learning Curve $17.99) There's a big green lilypad that floats and holds three frogs, each of which squirts in a different way, and a "bug" with wings that spin when it's pulled through the water. 1 1/2 & up. (800) 747-2454.

■ Turtle Tower ★ PLATINUM AWARD

(Sassy $8) Three friendly turtles stack on a center post base that attaches to the side of the tub with two large suction cups. The turtles which have different size drain holes, are fun for pretend play as well as scooping and pouring water. The best part of the toy is the funnel in the center post that spins as water runs through it! One of the best tub toys we've seen in a long time! 1 & up. (800) 323-6336.

NOTABLE PREVIOUS WINNERS:

Bath Fun (Battat $25) 13-piece set comes with wall-hung bath tower, buckets, spinners, squirter, and ducky. A great birthday present. 1 1/2 & up. Platinum Award '98. (800) 247-6144. **Fish Wheel** (Ambi $17) Pour water into the top and the water wheel will make the three red-and-yellow fish spin. Combines pouring with small lessons in cause and effect (310) 645-9680.

Basic Furniture

Tables and Chairs

This is a basic piece of gear that will be used for years of snacks, art projects, and tea parties. Best bets are going to have steady legs and a washable surface. After that, it's a matter of budget and style to fit your home. Check the underside of tables and chairs for smooth finishes that won't snag little fingers. Twos also enjoy a rocking or arm chair scaled to their size. 2 & up.

Some basic safety and design questions you may want to check:

Can your child get on and off chairs/bench easily?

Is this a set that will work when your child gets a little bigger?

If you're looking at a wooden set, are there exposed screws or nuts (check the underside) that can cut your child?

Is the surface washable and ready for abuse? (A beautiful painted piece will be destroyed by paint, play-dough, crayons, etc.)

Comparison Shopper— Plastic Folding Tables

This year both Fisher Price and Little Tikes introduced foldable plastic tables. Little Tikes **Easy Store Table** ($59.99) rectangular table is easier to fold away. However, testers report that Fisher-Price's round **Grow-With-Me**

Patio Table ($55) is easier for smaller children to use. Little Tikes model requires kids to step over the plastic that connects the bench to the table. Fisher-Price has no such barrier, making it easier for toddlers to use independently. Fisher-Price (800) 432-5437 / Little Tikes (800) 321-0183.

Selecting Backyard Gym Sets

Toward our goal of keeping you up-to-date in all areas of play, this section is updated to reflect new guidelines and choices. Buying a backyard gym is an investment in years of active fun that calls for care before you buy, as well as proper installation, maintenance, and supervision. Having such equipment right outside your own door provides an open-ended invitation to get out and use those muscles and that endless energy. Although the primary attraction may be the swing and slide, often these hold less long-term interest than the playhouse/climber, which is used for exercising both body and imagination.

Here are some tips on choosing equipment, installing it, and supervising its use.

Shop where you can see and compare gym sets that are set up. Ask yourself:

⚠ Is the set sturdy?

⚠ If it's wooden, is it smooth or likely to turn splintery? Is it made with pressure-treated wood? If so, you should know that the Consumer Safety Commission now reports that the quantity of chemicals used is not considered hazardous.

⚠ Whether it's wood, metal, or plastic, are there sharp or rough edges?

⚠ Are the swing seats like soft straps that conform to a child's body? These are safer and easier to get on and off.

⚠ If swings are hung on chains, are they sealed in vinyl so they won't pinch fingers?

⚠ Are the spaces between ladder rungs wide enough so a child's head can't get caught? All openings should be at least 9". Avoid sets with climbing bars that run the length of the set above the swings.

⚠ Is the bottom of the slide no more than 12" off the ground?

⚠ Are nuts and bolts embedded so they can't snag fingers and clothing?

⚠ Is the set scaled to your child's physical and developmental needs? Many sets come with climbers and slides that are not really appropriate for preschoolers. Do platforms have guardrails?

⚠ What's the weight capacity recommended by the manufacturer?

⚠ Who will install the set and how will it be anchored? Sets should be installed with stakes or in concrete "footings" so they won't tip, and on surfaces such as sand or wood chips 6"–12" deep to cushion falls. Grass is no longer considered safe enough for falls.

⚠ Do you really have room for it? Equipment should be at least six feet from fences, buildings, or anything that could endanger kids.

⚠ What's your budget? Most of the basic wooden sets start at $500, but that's just for the basic unit. After adding a slide, climber, and/or playhouse you're talking about $1,000 and up.

Here are the names of several major gym set companies:

⚠ **Childlife.** Top-rated. Distinctive wooden green finish is smoother and less likely to splinter than the cedar and pine gyms used in many other sets. $450 and up. (800) 462-4445.

⚠ **Rainbow Play Systems.** Steel parts are vinyl dipped, wood is chemical-free, built of redwood & cedar. Cadillac of gym sets, starts at $1100 & up. (800) 724-6269.

⚠ **Hedstrom** and **Roadmaster.** Metal sets from $149 and up. Available from Sears and many toy supermarkets.

⚠ **Little Tikes.** Their plastic **SkyCenter Playhouse Climber** ($650) has an attachable metal swing set extension that also needs to be anchored with concrete for stability. 3 & up. (800) 321-0183.

Best Travel Toys For Toddlers

- Familiar huggable
- Big washable crayons and pad of paper in a travel sack small enough to fit into a glove compartment
- Inflatable ball
- Small cardboard books they can handle themselves when in their car seats
- Musical toy or tape player and tapes
- For extended stays: a small set of big plastic blocks or the "favorite toy of the week," one you know she'll be happy to play with while you're unpacking!

Best Second Birthday Gifts For Every Budget

Under $100   **Fire Truck for Two** (Little Tikes) or **Sandbox** (Little Tikes/Step 2)

Under $75   **Toy Kitchen** or **First Climber** (Little Tikes)

Under $50   **Follow-the-Lights Talking Phone** (Mattel) or **Load & Ride Dump Truck** (Little Tikes) or **Snuffles** (Gund)

Under $30   **Duplo School Bus** (Lego) or **Yum Yum Cookie Monster** (Tyco) or **Bath Fun** (Battat)

Under $25   **Doll's Pram** (Little Tikes) or

                    Bigger Family Construction Wagon (Step 2)

Under $20	**Ball Tower** (Tomy/International Playthings) or **Fish Wheel** (Ambi) or **Push'n'Puff Vac** (Fisher-Price)
Under $15	**Stack'n'Build Choo Choo** (Fisher-Price) or **Pretend & Play Set** (Learning Resources) or **Groovy Girls** (Manhattan Toy)
Under $10	**Turtle Tower** (Sassy) **Crayola Big Bucket** or **Rock'n'Stack** (Lego Primo)
Under $5	**Play-Doh** (Hasbro)

A Word about Balloons: Despite the fact that latex balloons are considered unsafe for children under six, people continue to give them to kids in stores, parks and at parties. The problem is that kids can suffocate on pieces of latex if they bite and/or inhale a balloon they break or try to blow up. Yes, they are an old tradition—but a dangerous one. Why take the risk? Stick to Mylar!

3 • Preschool
Three to Four Years

What to Expect Developmentally

Learning Through Pretend. Preschoolers are amazing learning machines! Watch and listen to them at play and you can hear the wheels of their busy minds working full tilt. From sunup to sundown, preschoolers love playing pretend games. Playing all sorts of roles gives kids a chance to become big and powerful people. Providing props for such play gives kids the learning tools to develop language, imagination, and a better understanding of themselves and others.

Social Play. Your once-happy-to-be-only-with-you toddler has blossomed into a much more social being. She enjoys playing with other kids. Sharing is still an issue, but there's a budding understanding of give and take.

Solo Play. Unlike the toddler who moved from one thing to another, preschoolers become able to really focus their attention on building a bridge of blocks, working on a puzzle, or painting pictures.

Toys and Development. Although preschoolers love to play at counting and singing or even trying to write the alphabet, informal play is still the best path to learning. Building a tower with blocks, they discover some very basic math concepts. Digging in the sand or floating leaves in puddles, they make early science discoveries.

Big Muscles. Threes and fours also need time and space to run and climb and use their big muscles to develop coordination and a sense of themselves as able doers.

Your Role in Play. A child who has shelves full of stuffed animals or every piece of the hottest licensed character may seem to have tons of toys, but the truth is that, no matter how many trucks or dolls a kid has, such collections offer just one kind of play. Take an inventory of your child's toy clutter to see what's really being played with and what needs to be packed away or donated.

GEAR CHECKLIST FOR PRESCHOOLERS

✓ Set of blocks and props (small vehicles, animals, people)
✓ Trike
✓ Dolls and/or soft animals
✓ Dress-up clothes
✓ Housekeeping toys
✓ Transportation toys
✓ Matching games
✓ Picture books
✓ Sand and water toys
✓ Art materials—crayons, paints, clay
✓ Simple puzzles (eight pieces and up)
✓ Tape player and music and story tapes

Toys to Avoid

These toys pose a safety hazard:
✓ Electric toys or those that heat up with light bulbs that can burn
✓ Toys with projectile parts that can injure eyes
✓ Toys without volume control that can damage ears
✓ Two-wheelers with training wheels
✓ Latex balloons

These toys are developmentally inappropriate:
✓ Complex building sets that adults must build while children watch
✓ Teaching machines that reduce learning to a series of right or wrong answers
✓ Coloring books that limit creativity

Pretend Play

This is the age when pretend play blossoms. Some kids pretend with blocks, trains, and miniatures they move around as they act out little dramas. Others prefer dressing up and playing roles with their whole bodies. Either way, such games are more than fun. They help children learn to stretch their imaginations, try on powerful new roles, cope with feelings and fears, and develop language and social skills.

Dress-Up Play and Let's-Pretend Props

There are a lot of dress-up kits around. Truth be told, most kids enjoy dressing up in real clothes as much as the store-bought variety. Old pocketbooks, briefcases, jewelry, hats, and such are treasures to kids. For very specific role-playing, a hat, a scarf, or a homemade badge is often all that's needed to transform young players. Below are a few specialty items you may want to buy.

■ Construction Worker & Fire Chief ⚡99⚡

(Small World $15 each) Testers liked this orange vest with wooden Stop & Go traffic sign for serious road work and the Yellow slicker Fire Chief's coat with whistle. Hats are sold separately. Outfits in the Grow Ups collection are cut for kids who are not big for their age. (310) 645-9680.

■ Create-a-Fireman & Dress-a-Police ⚡99⚡

(Creative Education of Canada $25–$30) With all sorts of silvery Velcro badges, golden stars & buttons and belts, either of these well-made costumes will see plenty of action. Both come with hats and accessories

like whistles and handcuffs. We wish the packaging said "Firefighter."
3–7. Still top-rated: **Create-a-Crown** ($12), an adjustable crown with
gems that Velcro on for the young royal in your midst. Platinum Award
1998. Also **Create-A-Vest, Cape or Skirt.** (800) 982-2642.

■ Li'l Mail Carrier ⭐99⭐

(Fisher-Price $9.99) Our tester loved the stamp dispenser
on this blue mailbag. Has wipe-off postcards kids can
write on. A slot for a plastic "stamp" is not as good as
licking and sticking—but it's clever and develops
dexterity of another kind. 3 & up. (800) 432-5437.

Doctor's Gear

Comparison Shopper— Doctor's & Vet's Kits ⭐99⭐

Doctors no longer make house calls and even the traditional little black bag from Fisher-Price is gone this season. Their new version comes with a larger plastic case that is difficult to refill with all the equipment once it's emptied. **Sesame Street Doctor's Kit** *(Tyco $18) comes with a blue bag that doesn't work as well as the original black bag. (800) 488-8697. The basic gear in both is almost the same. For even more props, Battat's* **Medical Kit** *($25) is amazing—with all the usual tools plus scrubs, a mask, and a beeper (with a loud sound)! Comes in a big white attaché case (slide catches are slightly tricky). 3 & up. (800) 247-6144. For a working* **Stethoscope** *(Constructive Playthings $7.95). #MTC 261. (800) 832-0572.*

■ Nature Sounds Lantern ⭐99⭐

(Fisher-Price $9.99) A clever night light lantern with a sound button
that turns on the crickets, frogs, and owls without any of the discomfort of sleeping bags or mosquitoes! 3 & up. (800) 432-5437.

■ Cabbage Patch Kids Check-up Center

(Mattel $28) A small doll comes with "x-ray" machine, props for taking temps, listening to heartbeats, and getting shots. Testers liked the case that opens into an examination table. African-American doll available. (800) 524-5437.

■ Traveling Animal Vet Center

(Little Tikes $18) For on-the-go pets that
need a vet, here's a carrier and accessories. Although the box shows a kit-
ten, the print tells that no soft animal is included. Hard to assemble,
but a hit with testers. 3 & up. (800)
321-0183.

Housekeeping Tools

*Both girls and boys use props for cleaning, cooking, and
childcare. Kitchen toys will be used for playing house
and running restaurants. As children's experiences
broaden, so does the scope of their games of make-
believe. For more kitchens and toy dishes, see
Toddler section.*

■ Broom and Mop Set

Few toys will get more use by both boys and
girls than a mini-broom or mop. This is an inexpensive favorite that
you'll find in most toy supermarkets. Just check for smooth finish.
Battat has well-made plastic sets (800) 247-6144.

■ Shop & Cook Kitchen ♥99 PLATINUM AWARD

(Fisher-Price $64.99) This combo toy with store and
cash register on one side and a kitchen on the other
is loaded with play value. Done in gender-free
primary colors, this can be passed from sister
to brother. Comes with accessories and a
"working" sink—you can actually put water
in it and then lift and dump. Note: We
were unable to get the screws in all the way,
but the toy holds together. 3 & up. **Price
Check Shopping Cart** ($22.99) also looked
like fun but was not ready for testing. (800) 432-5437.

■ Musical Cake Surprise ♥99

(Fisher-Price $14.99) Our testers loved this
novelty plastic cake that flips from a wed-
ding cake to a birthday cake. The special
candle or bride and groom trigger the
cake to play "Happy Birthday" or "Here

Comes the Bride." Comes with dishes, a cake server, and forks. Use as a fun intro to fractions! Takes 2 AA batteries. 2 1/2–5. (800) 432-5437.

Play Phones: *See Toddlers Chapter*

Dolls and Huggables

Preschoolers love soft animals as huggable playmates. In addition to large stuffed animals, a baby doll is the perfect play companion for trips away from home and for at-home tea parties.

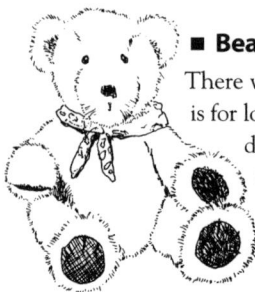

■ **Bears of the Year** 🏆

There were so many great choices this year. The trend is for long-limbed bears with plush that looks pre-cuddled, such as **Slippers** (North American Bear $20) or **Belly** (Gund $15). Our top favorite, **Sassafras** 🏆 PLATINUM AWARD (Manhattan Toy $20), has jointed limbs, a bandanna scarf, silky-soft body, and a sweet face. Also top-rated, **Schlepp** 🏆 or **BeanBottom** (Gund $15 each), with round bottoms and understuffed, floppy feel; & **Butterscotch** (Gund $24 & up), a taffy-colored bear with shaggy hair and long snout. The classic **Curious George** (Gund $25) is always a favorite for 4 & up. Gund (732) 248-1500 / North American Bear (800) 682-3427 / Manhattan Toy (800) 747-2454.

■ **Babybear Doll** 🏆

(North American Bear Co. $48) Technically a bear, but it's so much more. Comes dressed in a blue checked romper. Bring home in felt bassinet with bunting ($30). Bottle and pacifier sold separately ($10). Smaller versions also available. Very, very special. (800) 682-3427.

■ **Les Minis Calins**

(Corolle $15 & up) These adorable floppy little 8" dolls have bean-bag bodies and can be used with a **baby carrier** ($12) or **spring chair** ($16) for added play power. Also trés jolie for a birthday gift, one doll comes with two outfits in a **wicker carrying case** ($50). Platinum Award '97. 3 & up. If you're looking for an anatomically correct doll, **Fan-Fan** boy or girl drink-and-wet dolls

($80) are pricey but lovable and tubbable. (800) 628-3655.

Favorite Characters:

■ Arthur & D.W. 🌟

(Eden & Playskool) Arthur continues to be very popular. Our favorite this year is **D.W.** ($24) & her **ballet set** ($14) that comes with tutu, a less-than-permanent paper crown, and slippers. A charming gift for dance recitals. (800) 443-4275. Playskool's **Dress Me Arthur & D.W.** ($18 each) have clothes with zippers, snaps, buttons, and ties. Arthur's glasses may be especially attractive to kids who wear glasses. 3–6. (800) 752-9755.

■ Rugrats Collection 🌟

(Mattel $20 & up) If you have a Rugrats fan at home, these novelty dolls will be a hit. Our favorites are Spike the dog, with ears that go up in the air, and Angelica, with twirling pigtails. New for '99, soft-bodied Slumber Party versions. 4–8. (800) 524-TOYS.

■ Dressable Madeline Doll BLUE CHIP

(Eden $30) Oo-la-la! That's what any Madeline fan will say who receives a 15" soft doll that seems to step right out of the storybook (complete with appendix scar). Soft and huggable, she has an amazing wardrobe available, like her green coat with gray woolly collar, hat, and skates outfit. ($15). Bring home the books & videos, too. 4 & up. (800) 443-4275.

Interactive Dolls

■ ActiMates Barney

(Microsoft $99) Barney's arrival last year marked a new chapter in high-tech interactive dolls. It remains the most magical of its kind because it was expertly designed to match the skills of its preschool audience. Barney not only sings, plays games, and engages players in active give-and-take—he also inter-acts with the VCR and the computer (see Computer

chapter). Takes 6 AA batteries. 2 1/2 & up. Platinum '98. (800) 426-9400. While this year's new **Arthur** and **D.W.** are marked for 4 & up, the skills the dolls work on (telling time, rhyming words, repeating tongue twisters, and even saying the ABCs backwards) are more appropriate for 1st and 2nd graders. Other new dolls that interact with computers, **Big Bird** (Tyco) and **Pooh** (Mattel), were not ready for testing.

■ Talking Playtime Big Bird

(Tyco $30) For a still magical but less expensive doll, we recommend Big Bird, who plays "peek-a-boo," "patty-cake," and "This Little Piggy." We'd say older 2s, 3s, and 4s. Comes with 3 AA batteries. Platinum '98. We also preferred **Yum Yum Cookie Monster** (see Toddlers) to the new **Toss & Tickle Me Elmo** who giggles and yells, "Yowee!" when you follow his plea to "Toss Elmo!" Truth be told, this is a pretty heavy toy to toss—it does not tickle if it hits you! See **Elmo & his Puppy** in Toddler chapter (800) 488-8697.

■ Hug & Learn Little Leap

(Leap Frog $39.99) For a really smart talking plush huggable, we like this big green frog that not only knows how to count and say its ABCs, it also says "please" and "thank you"! There are several modes of play here. Kids can push Leap's shirt and he says letters, or they can play in search mode that teaches letter names and sounds. A third game looks for letters and numbers that come before and after. This is one of the cleverest dolls of its kind and will be enjoyed by 5s and 6s who are still working on these skills. Takes 4 AA batteries. They say 2–5, we say 4 & up. Also, fun for naming animals and playing little games of logic, **Think & Go Zoo** ($29.99). (800) 701-5327.

Multicultural Dolls

Just a few years ago, **Cabbage Patch Kids** (Mattel) were almost alone in this category. They are still a good affordable choice, but happily there are now more options in all price ranges. Olmec ($15 each) has both Hispanic and African-American dolls that are available in toy supermar-

kets. (800) 677-6966. The Pleasant Company's **Bitty Baby Dolls** *($38 each) are 15" soft-bodied dolls available with Caucasian, African-American, Asian-American, or Hispanic features and skin tones. Platinum Award '96. (800) 845-0005.*

Comparison Shopper— Doll Strollers and Furniture

Budget and taste will go into making the choices here. Just like the real equipment, there are doll carriers for the silver-spoon set and more practical models for your average doll.

Doll Buggy

(Little Tikes $25) A gender-specific pink and white plastic carriage that can hold a doll up to 18". 2 & up. Little Tikes' **Shopping Cart** ($25) fills the bill for a gender-free, more open-ended prop with a doll seat. (800) 321-0183.

■ **5-in-1 Deluxe Doll Nursery**

(Little Tikes $40) A double doll changer comes with two highchairs on either end and a place to bathe and change the babies in between. We could do without all that pink, but our testers enjoyed playing and exchanging baby stories! (800) 321-0183.

■ **Wooden Doll Cradle** BLUE CHIP

(Community Playthings $90) A solid maple cradle designed for schools and built to last. The large 29" model is big enough so kids can climb in and play baby or put a family of dolls to sleep. Sure to become a family heirloom. 2 & up. #C140. (800) 777-4244.

Puppets and Puppet Stages

Through the mouths of puppets, kids can say things that they might not otherwise speak about, so puppets are a way of venting feelings and developing imagination and language skills. Young puppeteers replay stories, create original ones, and develop skills that link to reading and writing. Animal puppets from Gund and Applause are widely available. Since kids know familiar characters from Sesame Street (Applause) and Disney (Gund), it's easy for young pup-

peteers to step into familiar roles. Gund (732) 248-1500 / Applause (800) 777-6990. See Early School Years for more puppets and stages.

■ Family Puppet Sets

(Constructive Playthings $24.95 per set) For realistic role-playing, try this four-piece family with Mom, Dad, brother, and sister. Caucasian, Hispanic, African-American, and Asian American sets available. All-fabric heads and bodies. Company will customize families! #FPH721L. (800) 832-0572.

■ Royal Rascals Puppets

(Manhattan Toy Co. $9 each) Retelling most folktales calls for some regal puppets like these 8" velour royals. (800) 747-2454.

■ Finger Puppet Gloves

(Alex $7) Adult storytelling may be enhanced with a glove that has finger puppets to fit on each digit. Good for waiting room or travel, choose from several different story gloves; **Red Riding Hood** & **Three Bears.** 3 & up. (800) 666-2539.

■ Tabletop Puppet Theatre

(Alex $30) You can easily set up this 24"W x 22"H x 9"D wooden puppet stage without any tools. It's a sturdy wooden stage that's stable and good for small scale productions. A larger floor model ($70) 48" high with chalk surface for messages. 3 & up, up, up. (800) 666-2539.

> **FREEBIE: Do it yourself—a large appliance box can be turned into an excellent puppet stage, and so can a cloth-covered card table that kids can hide behind. Another great option is a spring curtain rod and length of fabric that can be used in any doorway.**

Pretend Settings: Mountain, Doll Houses, and Parking Garage

Some of the mini-settings listed in the Toddlers section will be used in more elaborate ways now. If you put them away, try bringing them out again and see how differently your child plays with them. Here are descriptions of recommended settings that are more complex.

■ **Adventure Mountain Raceway**

(Little Tikes $45) Few toys have gotten more raves than this multi-tracked mountain with six different courses for little cars to race down. Trains can be fed through tunnels in the base. Comes with two die-cast cars. Keep this on the floor or cars may fly off into kids' faces. Great group toy. 3 & up. Platinum Award '96. (800) 321-0183.

Doll Houses 🌟

Dollhouses should be kept simple for little hands. That's what we liked about the Little Tikes Place, which is no longer available. **Grand Dollhouse** *(Fisher-Price $64.99) This 3 story fold-up house with detailed furnishings is a better choice for old 4s & beyond. This year there's a home office and sets of Asian, African-American, Hispanic, or Caucasian families. For a smaller more portable version,* **Family Vacation Camper** *(Fisher-Price $31) looked promising but wasn't available for testing. (800) 432-5437. Simpler, with a more open plan,* **Wooden Doll House** *(Plan Toys $99 & $139). Choose either of their modern-looking A-frames with open roofs for easy access. The pricier one has sliding doors and wallpaper. Furnishings for bedroom, bath, living room, and kitchen are beautifully crafted in wood. ($20 per room). (310) 645-9680.*

■ **Big Action Garage**

(Fisher-Price $50) This 28" high garage is so much better than the smaller version from the same maker. A four-story parking garage with elevator lifts lowers and opens on each floor so cars can make their way down the twisting ramps. 3 & up. Platinum Award '97. (800) 432-5437.

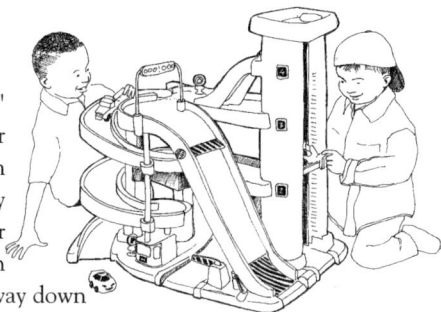

■ **Farm House** 🌟

(Battat $45) Larger and more elaborate than most, this big red barn with carrying handle opens to reveal a double-sided two-story barn with windows, gates, working doors, and plenty of barnyard critters.

Good for language and pretend play. 3 & up. (800) 247-6144.

■ Little People Mainstreet 💯

(Fisher-Price $29.99) Not just a car wash, restaurant, pet shop, barber shop, or heliport—it's all of these places with vehicles and Little People for a cityscape pretend. 3 & up. (800) 432-5437.

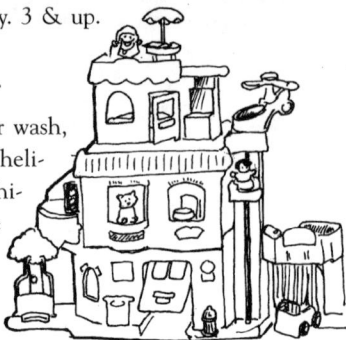

Trucks and Other Vehicles

Preschoolers are fascinated with all forms of transportation. The real things are out of reach and on the move, but toy trucks, cars, boats, jets, and trains are ideal for make-believe departures, both indoors and out. Choose vehicles with working parts to use with blocks, in the sandbox, or at the beach. Blue Chip choices such as Matchbox cars or Hot Wheels are now appropriate and are often the first "collectible."

■ Construction Truck with Hard Hat 💯

(Little Tikes $20) This is a showy yet relatively inexpensive toy that will be enjoyed for dramatic play indoors or out. Little Tikes vehicles are articulated for easy action and made to withstand sand and water at beach or sandbox. Choose a working dump truck or loader. 3 & up. (800) 321-0183.

■ Mighty Tonka Dump Truck BLUE CHIP

(Tonka $17) and **Mighty Backhoe** ($25) are updates of the ones you probably played with and have more details for older kids. (800) 248-6652.

First Trains and Track Toys

What They Learn

A non-electric train is a classic toy that will keep growing in complexity as you add working bridges, roundhouses, and other extras. (Note: Preschoolers are not ready for electric trains, except to watch!)

Trains are really open-ended puzzles with no right or wrong answers. Making the track work often becomes more important to many kids than actually playing with the trains.

Many stores display their trains on tabletops with track glued down, but much of the open-ended play value is lost when you do that at home. Making ever-changing settings is half the fun. Skip the table and invest in more tracks and bridges.

Train-Buying Tips

Most starter sets come with just a circle of track that will lose its appeal quickly. Start out with enough tracks to make it interesting. Most wooden track sets are compatible with Brio trains, the best-known line. For economy and multiple choices, add accessories from various makers.

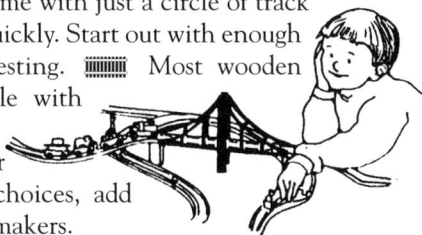

Good starter sets

■ Intermediate Suspension Bridge Train Set

(Brio $76) Brio's top-of-the-line wooden train set has 18 pieces of track (135"), one suspension bridge that looks like the Golden Gate, ascending tracks, and a three-piece train. Platinum Award '94. (888) 274-6869.

■ Wooden Train

(T. C. Timber $79.75) Set comes with 37 pieces—enough track to form a figure eight, a tunnel-bridge, trees, and four-piece train. (800) 245-7622.

■ Thomas The Tank Engine 🏆

(Learning Curve $99) Thomas fans will be thrilled with the 50-piece set that includes 3 trains, tunnel, barrel loader, a shed, signs, trees, and play figures. Note: Some Thomas trains are too tall for other makers' bridges. Also great & less pricey, a figure 8 set with one tunnel/bridge ($40). (800) 704-8697.

Best New Wooden Train Props ⭐99⭐

New accessories can inspire fresh layouts and keep interest chugging along.

■ Suspension Bridge ⭐99⭐

(Learning Curve $49.99) Even the most jaded train buff will say WOW! This elegant suspension bridge has flexible tracks, green suspension "wires," and brick arches. Putting this together is not hard, but challenging. 5 & up. (800) 704-8697.

■ Curved Viaduct ⭐99⭐

(Learning Curve $44.99) Four arched and curved pieces with "stone-work" decals connect to form an amazing raised viaduct for wooden trains to cross. This does not come with ascending track, although your builder will need them. A beauty! (800) 704-8697.

■ Sky Bridge ⭐99⭐

(Brio $55) Lots of high bridges for wooden trains with tricky descending tracks are too hard for beginners to build. This two-piece bridge goes together with ease and has a center tunnel underpass wide enough for a double track. 3 & up. (888) 274-6869.

■ Sawmill with Dumping Depot ⭐99⭐

(Learning Curve $60) This elaborate setting has a working "saw" that dumps and splits a log with a spring loader and buzzing sound. No sharp parts, but complex action. (800) 704-8697.

SAFETY TIP: Many toy train sets come with very small accessories (trees, people, and animals) and the trains also have small parts. They are not appropriate for toddlers or even preschoolers who still mouth their toys.

Construction Toys

If there's one toy no child should be without, blocks are it! Few toys are more basic. Stacking a tower, balancing a bridge, setting up a zoo—all call for imagination, dexterity, decision making, and problem solving. Built into the play are early math and language concepts that give concrete meaning to abstract words like "higher," "lower," "same," and "different." Best of all, blocks are wonderfully versatile—they build a space city today, a farm tomorrow.

Kids will enjoy both wood and plastic types of blocks, which encourage different kinds of valuable play experiences. Choosing blocks depends largely on your budget and space. Although many of these sets are pricey, they are a solid investment that will be used for years to come.

Wooden Blocks

Unit blocks come in many shapes and lengths, all carefully proportioned to each other. Many catalogs offer unit blocks in sets of different sizes. Parents are sometimes disappointed when kids don't use the small starter sets they buy. Keep in mind that kids really can't do much with a set of 20 blocks and no props. This is one of those items where the more they have, the more they can do.

■ Master Builder Block System

(T. C. Timber $25 & up) These wooden blocks are 40 percent smaller than regular unit blocks but maintain their size relationships. Most interesting in this system are architectural sets: **Middle Eastern, Antiquity, Romantic, Medieval, Russian,** and **Japanese.** Platinum Award '96. (800) 245-7622.

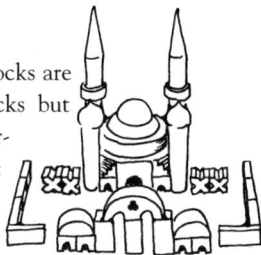

> ### 🛍 Comparison Shopper—Unit Blocks
> *No two catalogs have the same number of blocks or shapes in any set, so there's a small difference in all the sets listed. The cost of shipping will vary depending upon where you live, and the weight and price of the item. Our best suggestion is that you call around and compare. Here's a sampling of*

what a good basic set will run:

Back to Basics set of 82 blocks in 16 shapes. (#133). $124 (800) 356-5360.

T. C. Timber set with 87 pieces in 23 shapes. (#50-6674). $225 (800) 245-7622.

(Higher price reflects greater number of shapes with architectural accessories.)

Constructive Playthings set of 85 pieces in 15 shapes. (#CP-U30SL). $169 (800) 832-0572.

Grand Rivers: Super Set of 101 dark hardwood blocks with 88 pieces in 16 shapes plus a 7-piece Roman arch and 6 classical columns. (#A60). $88 (800) 567-5600.

Props for Blocks

Providing a variety of props, such as small-scaled vehicles, animals, and people, enhances building and imaginative play. Here are some props designed to inspire young builders. Our favorites:

■ Rainbow Blocks

(Guidecraft $48.95) Kids will love looking through these 14 smooth hardwood blocks with "window" panels of colored Plexiglas. Scaled to unit blocks, there are rectangles, triangles, arches, and squares. Pricey but special for adding accent shapes to constructions. (800) 555-6526.

■ Mini Traffic Signs

(Guidecraft $12) Six wooden signs come in a neat carrying case. 4 & up. (800) 544-6526.

■ Drawbridge Gate

(T.C. Timber) for small or unit blocks ($16 & up). (800) 245-7622.

■ Windows and Door Blocks

(Constructive Playthings $16.95) Scaled to fit standard unit blocks: a five piece set of 4 windows and one door. (#PCR-62L). (800) 832-0572.

Q ACTIVITY TIP – Playful Cleanup: Preschoolers often need help cleaning up. You can get some learning in by saying, "I'll find the trucks, you pick up all the cars," or "Let's find all the smallest blocks

first." Set up open shelves for blocks and baskets
for props to avoid having a constant jumbled mess!

Cardboard Blocks
See Toddler Chapter

Plastic Blocks
*Plastic building sets call for a different kind of dexterity. Here's
what you should look for:*

Beginners are better off with larger pieces that
make bigger and quicker constructions.

Encourage beginning builders to experiment
rather than copy or watch you build.

■ Duplo X-Large Bucket
(Lego $19) A tub full of chunky plastic Duplo building blocks to fill
and dump, snap together, and take apart. Small sets are good for add-
ons, but be sure to start with a large enough set. 1 1/2–5. For more
advanced builders, **Lego Freestyle sets** designed for 4s & up. (800)
233-8756.

■ Children's Zoo 🏆
(Lego Systems $25) Lions, tigers, elephants,
oh my! A classic set just right for adding
pretend punch to a set of Duplos. Comes
with a merry go round and zoo keeper.
Also, **Duplo Playtable** 🏆 ($20) comes
with 20 blocks. (800) 233-8756.

■ Multi-Activity Table
(Nilo $200) This Cadillac of play tables (33" x 48" x 20") is a piece
of wooden furniture that's more versatile than most with a raised edge
to hold everything from train tracks to building blocks. (800) 872-
6456.

> **SHOPPING TIP: Older preschoolers will enjoy mix-
> ing their old chunky Duplos with the smaller-
> scaled Lego bricks. These do demand more dexterity, so
> don't rush kids into frustration. See Early School Years
> Chapter for more advanced sets.**

■ Mega Blocks BLUE CHIP

(Mega Blocks $10 & up) These oversized plastic pegged blocks are easy for preschoolers to take apart, fit together, and assemble into B-I-G constructions with a minimum of pieces. Select a set with wheels and angled pieces for more flexibility. (800) 465-6342.

Early Games

Preschoolers are not ready for complex games with lots of rules or those that require strategy, math, or reading skills. Best bets for family fun are games of chance such as lotto, picture dominoes, and classics such as Candyland, where players depend upon the luck of the draw rather than skill. Taking turns is often hard, and so is the concept of winning or losing. We've selected games that can be played cooperatively and those that are quick and short so there can be lots of winners. Some of the best games here can also be played as solitaire matching games.

Active Games

■ Blue's Clues TV Play-Along Game Kit 🏅

(Eden $16) Fans of Blue's Clues can make up their own hide-and-find game with three blue paws to hide and their own handy-dandy note-book—just like Steve's. They'll also have a small velour Blue of their own. 3 & up. (800) 443-4275.

■ Footloose

(Ravensburger $19.95) An unusually physically active game that includes having to do jumping jacks, hugs, and sit-ups to get to win. No reading needed. 2–6 players. 3 & up. (800) 445-8347.

■ Hot Potato

(Parker Brothers $14.99) Squeeze this soft, electronic, musical talking spud to turn on his sound. Pass him around fast! If you're holding him when he yells "Yahoo!" you take a hot card. Three cards and you're out. A fast, fun game for two or more players. Platinum Award '97. 4 & up.

Color, Counting, and Dominoes

■ Busytown Board Game

(Ravensburger $19.95) Can't stand another round of Candyland? Here, players roll a color die and move ahead to the matching color. Roll a "gold bug" and be sent ahead or back. Remove the picture card of Lowly that sends players back to the start—something few preschoolers can deal with well. Takes 10 min. 2–6 players. 3–6. Also top-rated, **Curious George Match-a-Balloon** and **Maisy Dominoes Game** (800) 445-8347.

■ Farm Animals To Go!

(Learning Resources $11.95) Try a game of "Four-in-a-Row Bingo" or the "Put-'em-in-a-Pen" sorting game. Forty-eight pleasing-to-handle playing pieces, number and color cubes, and several wonderful early learning games for sorting, making patterns, and memory. Right on the mark for preschoolers. 3–5. (800) 222-3909.

■ Jumbo Domino

(Edushape $19.95) 14 giant vinyl dominoes with dots, pictures, or geometric shapes. Fun for matching games on the floor or even in the tub, since these float and stick to bathroom tiles. 3 & up. (800) 404-4744.

■ Fishin' Around ✪99✪

(Milton Bradley $19.99) Our testers enjoyed the novelty of this motorized musical fish-catching game that develops counting, matching, and eye-hand coordination. We wish there were a volume control. 4–7.

■ Maisy Game

(Briarpatch $20) Players spin and pick up sturdy cardboard cutouts to match color, pattern, and objects on their picture board of Maisy. Develops language and matching skills. 3–6. Platinum Award '95. 3–7. (800) 232-7427.

Matching and Memory

■ Goodnight Moon Game
✪99✪ PLATINUM AWARD

(Briarpatch $19.95) This utterly simple, but right-on-the-mark, game features illustrations from M. W. Brown's classic *Goodnight Moon*. Children take turns pick-

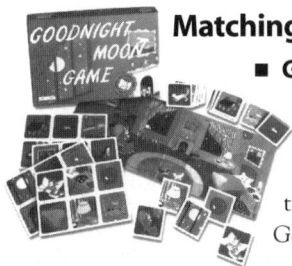

ing and matching cards with pictures on their lotto-style playing boards. Good choice for developing language and visual skills. No reading or counting. 1–4 players. 2 1/2–6. (800) 232-7427.

■ I SPY Preschool Game 🏆

(Briarpatch $14.95) Based on the wonderful I SPY books, this can be played solo or with a group. Players "read" the riddle cards with pictures of the objects that they must find within a bigger picture on a matching card. A terrific getting ready to read game. 4 & up. (800) 232-7427.

■ Itsy Bitsy Spider 🏆

(Discovery Toys $13) A fast-paced game for 2–4 players where the object is to get your spider to the top of drain by matching color or shape from the dice to the colors or shapes on your board. A good take-along toy. (800) 426-4777.

■ Lilly's Purple Plastic Purse 🏆

(Gamewright $19) Players use picture cards featuring Kevin Henkes' well loved character, Lilly, to make-up original stories. Then, one card is removed and storyteller must remember what's missing. Also top-rated, **Lilly's 3 For All** ($10) Three simple matching games that develop language and visual skills. 4 & up. (800) 638-7568.

■ Picture Pairs Matching Game

(Ravensburger $13.95) Lotto boards are sorted by toys, fruits, clothes, and other familiar objects to know and name. Players take turns pulling cards and matching them to board. A quick game for 1–6 players. Develops vocabulary, turn-taking, and visual matching skills. 3 & up. Also top-rated, **Wildlife Bingo.** (800) 445-8347.

Puzzles

A word about puzzles. Preschoolers gradually move from whole-piece puzzles to simple puzzles that challenge them to see how two or more parts make a whole.For kids with no previous experience, start with 5–7 pieces in a frame.Children's skills vary, so take your cue from the child.Some fours can handle 20–30 pieces of a jigsaw, while others are still working on 10–15 pieces. Large pieces are easier for little hands A word of warning: Most of the wooden puzzles that came our way this year were badly finished and were awash with splinters. Our best advice is stick to cardboard or vinyl.

■ Baby Animals

(Ravensburger $14.95) Fans of DK books will enjoy this 2' x 3' floor puzzle with 24 pieces that feature 21 baby animals. 4 & up. (800) 445-8347.

■ Big Bulldozer Giant Puzzle ★99★

(Frank Schaffer $14.95) Twenty-four big pieces make a giant 2' x 3' yellow bulldozer with pivot action. There are also three mini-puzzles (a female and male worker and a pile of bricks) There's no frame so making this shaped puzzle with almost all yellow pieces can be challenging for beginners. They say 3, but we'd say more like 4 & up. Also, **Big Red Barn** (31 pieces). (800) 421-5565.

■ Count With Maisy Puzzle

(Ravensburger $14.95) 24 giant pieces create a 2' x 3' floor puzzle with pictures of Maisy doing lots of things kids can count. A nice companion to the Maisy Alphabet puzzle. Says 2 & up; we'd say 3s & 4s. Platinum '98. Also top-rated, **Busy Town Puzzle** & **Lucy Cousins' Animals.** (800) 445-8347.

■ Firefighter ★99★

(Frank Schaffer $13.95) A giant 30-piece floor puzzle of a fire truck for naming and knowing. 4 & up. Also BLUE CHIP winner, **Number Train.** 3 & up. (800) 421-5565.

■ My Size Friends Puzzle ★99★

(Mattel $7.99) Kids were thrilled when they put these child-sized Pooh characters together with big cardboard pieces. Other Disney giant floor puzzles were not ready for testing. (800) 524-8697.

■ Sing-A-Long Puzzles ★99★

(Great American Puzzle Factory $11.95) Every year we see new novelties on preschool puzzles. Testers liked singing along after doing this 24-piece floor puzzle that plays "I've Been Working on the Railroad" with a push-button music box. 3 & up. (800) 922-1194.

Lacing Games

Stringing games help kids refine the fine motor eye-hand skills needed for writing. While stringing beads, they can also sort by color and make patterns, learning to see likes and differences. Three favorites: **Jumbo Stringing Beads** BLUE CHIP (T. C. Timber $20) 31 large wooden beads in different colors and shapes. (800) 245-7622. **Cotton Reels** (Galt $9) Big colorful plastic spools to sort and string. (800) 448-4258. **Lacing and Tracing Animals** (Lauri $6.50) Classic chipboard animal shapes to sew or draw. (800) 245-7622.

Science Toys and Activities

Floating a leaf in a puddle, collecting pebbles in the park, making mud pies in the sandbox, watching worms wiggle—these are a few of the active ways children learn about the natural world. Here are our favorites for early science exploration:

Magnets and Observation Tools

■ Magnetic Blocks BLUE CHIP

(Battat $13–16) Playful introduction to the power of magnetism. Magnets are safely embedded in 16 brightly colored blocks. Can be built into moving vehicles with wheels. (800) 247-6144.

■ My Big Magnet

(Battat $5) A giant horseshoe magnet. Easy to hold and powerful enough to pick up several metal objects. (800) 247-6144.

> **Q ACTIVITY TIP:** Give your preschooler a sheet of peel-off stickers to put on anything they find that the magnet sticks to. Or give kids a bag full of household items to sort in two baskets. Have them put all the things that are attracted to the magnet in one basket and all the others in another.

Garden Work

Preschoolers love the magic of seeing things grow. Apartment dwellers can garden on a windowsill. For the backyard set, more elaborate child-sized tools are available. **Plastic Garden Tools** (Little Tikes $13) are safer for preschoolers than scaled down metal *versions from other companies. An accidental swing in the wrong direction will not mean a trip to the ER. They also don't have splintery handles as some metal tools do, and won't rust when they are inevitably left outside..*

Garden Sets 🪴

Lawn & Garden Cart (Little Tikes $25) For young gardeners, this Blue Chip gardening cart has pockets that hold watering can, trowel, and cultivator. Unlike a tippy wheelbarrow, it has two front wheels for stable pushing action. Also recommended, plastic **Garden Tools** ($13 set of three) 2–6. (800) 321-0183. For somewhat bigger kids, **Tot Deluxe Garden Set** 🪴 (Battat $34) This blue wagon kids can push or pull comes with large sturdy plastic shovel, rake, hoe, sprinkling can, and hand tools for serious gardening. 3 & up. (800) 247-6144.

Lawn Mowers 🪴

Choose either the classic Little Tikes **Mulching Mower** *($25), Fisher-Price's* **Bubble mower,** *or Ertl's new* **Action Lawn Mower** *($26.99) from the John Deere collection. Pull-back handle makes a whirling sound as it "cuts" (too noisy for inside) and the see-through dome lets you see the grass inside. Little Tikes (800) 321-0183 / Ertl (800) 553-4886 / Fisher-Price (800) 432-5437.*

SAFETY TIP: Kids should be nowhere near real mowers in action. Flying pebbles travel at 200 mph and can cause deadly accidents. Ditto on riding with adults on power mowers!

■ Push/Pull Wagon

(Radio Flyer $60) Bigger than the classic red wagon, this plastic update has higher sides, a well, and a stout handle for pushing or pulling kids or cargo. This and the Blue Chip classic version are ideal for carting plants, tools, imaginary playmates—you name it. (800) 621-7613.

78

TOILETS

Sand, Water, & Bubble Toys

Sand and water are basic materials for exploring liquids and solids, floating and sinking, sifting and pouring. An inexpensive pail and shovel are basic gear and less upsetting to lose than the high-priced spread. A sand mill is also basic for sandbox or beach. Older preschoolers will be delighted with a set of turrets and tower molds for building beautiful sand castles—kids will add moat, imagination, and who knows what else! Some other sand tools are also worth considering.

■ Brio Waterway ⭐99

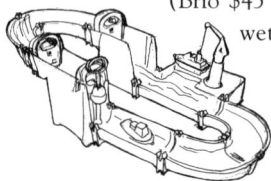

(Brio $45 & up) Learn how locks lift ships with this wet and entertaining hands-on waterway. We've seen waterways before, but this system goes together with greater ease and no leaks. An adult will need to assemble and supervise, but this is a great poolside, backyard water toy for 4–8s. (888) 274-6869.

> **SHOPPING TIP:** You can find molds in almost any toy store. Just be sure to check the edges for roughness. Most catalogs offer new combinations every season, some with handy net bags for storage.

■ New Giant Castle ⭐99

(Battat $30) Dreaming of castles rising by the sea? This 14-piece set is designed for a group with multi-sized towers, turrets, stairs, and tools for building amazing castles. All the pieces fit into a gigantic pail that's shaped like a royal gatehouse. All ages. Still top-rated, **Deluxe Sand & Water Set** (Battat $21) 14 pieces including a sandmill and hose sprinkler on the big bucket.(800) 247-6144.

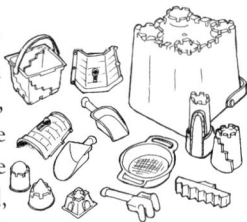

> **Q ACTIVITY TIP:** Give kids empty squeeze bottles, sieves, funnels, different-shaped cups, and tumblers for pouring, sprinkling, and spilling experiments.

Bubbles 🌟

*Blowing bubbles has come a long way from the small plastic con-
tainers of pink liquid with a small, sticky wand. For groups:*
The 12-Piece Bubble Party (*Battat $17*)
*includes wands, trumpets, giant rings,
and a waffle wand (enough pieces for
nine kids!). (800) 247-6144.* **The No-
Spill Big Bubble Bucket** (*Little Kids $13.99*) *has
three extra-large wands that can't get lost in the bottle!*
(800) 545-5437. New **Bubble Tumbler Minis** (*$6.99*) *makes a
great party favor. Also new,* **Koosh Bubbles Bubba Billions**
(*$9.99*) *makes tons of bubbles with a push of a button. Purists may
be disturbed by push button bubbles—but this is great for a crowd
of bubble chasers! 5 & up.*

> **Q** **ACTIVITY TIP: For super-large bubbles, mix 1 cup
of Dawn liquid detergent with 3 tablespoons of
Karo syrup in 2 1/2 quarts of cold water. Stir gently.
Leftovers (if you have any) need to be refrigerated.
Ideal for large groups.**

Portable Pools and Sandboxes
See Toddlers Section

Active Physical Play

*Active play builds preschoolers' big muscles, coordination, and con-
fidence in themselves as able doers. It also establishes healthy active
patterns for fitness, relieves stress, and provides a legitimate reason
to run and shout. Agreeing on the rules of the game and taking
turns promote important social and cooperative skills. For
tips on buying swing sets, see Toddlers section.*

■ Easy Score Basketball Set

(*Little Tikes $35*) This looks like the big kids'
hoop, but it's designed for the youngest slam-
dunkers. It not only adjusts from 2 1/2' to 4', the
hoop has an extra-wide back and a big backboard
to make scoring easier. Base can be filled with sand

for added stability. 2 & up. Platinum Award '97. (800) 321-0183.

■ 3-in-1 Baseball Trainer 🏷️

(Little Tikes $29.99) As kids grow, this baseball teaching tool goes from being a simple tee ball to a pop-up pitching machine. At first an adult steps on pedal to launch ball for young player to try to hit. Later player can remove tee and step on pedal to launch the ball independently. Comes with five balls and flat-sided bat for beginners. 4 & up. (800) 321-0183.

Beginner Balls 🏷️

Both **Gertie Balls** *(Small World $5 & up) and* **Yadda Balls** *(International Playthings $5 & up) are gummy inflatable balls that are soft enough for kids who may be scared of big heavy balls coming towards them. We particularly like the* **Yadda Football** *and the* **Nobbie Gertie.** *3 & up. Small World (310) 645-9680 / International Playthings (800) 445-8347.*

Comparison Shopper—Golf Sets 🏷️

Young Tigers-in-training have a variety of choices for teeing off.

Sure Putt Golf 🏷️ (Fisher-Price $9.99) A golfer's dream come true—the putting green in this set won't let your near-hits roll away—the Velcro surface grabs special balls that come close to a hole-in-one. Unlike most kids' golf sets, this has a pretty realistic putter. 3 & up. (800) 432-5437. Miniature golf aficionados will like the fantasy of the **Castle Kingdom** (Discovery Toys $35), a set of castles with turrets & towers for indoors or out. Says 3 & up—we'd say 4–7. (800) 426-4777. **Tournament Golf Set** (Little Tikes $25) has a no-nonsense look with three challenging putting greens. Comes with wedge, putter, and six balls for indoors or out. Says 2 & up. We'd say 4 & up. (800) 321-0183.

■ Big Ball Hopper

(Hedstrom $11.99) Hop-on balls are classics for active play and building coordination. This new version has colorful balls inside that bounce and make noise as child bounces on the big ball. Great for building big muscle action and coordination. This company's **Mega Balls** are also top-rated. 4 & up. (800) 765-9665.

■ Rocking Rider Horse

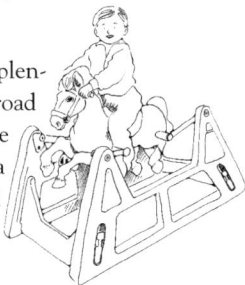

(Today's Kids $75 & up) A splendidly stable rocking horse with broad base and innovative rubber hinges that replace the usual metal springs. **Midnight Mustang,** a black stallion, comes with motion-activated horse sounds that can be turned off. 3 & up. (800) 258-8697.

Comparison Shopper— Water Sprinklers

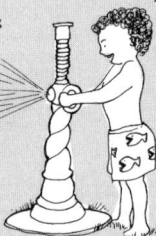

If you'd rather not have a hose that kids can spray at each other, consider **Waterpark Twist'n'Spout Sprinkler** (Little Tikes $25), a tall sprinkler with four different spray patterns including straight up in the air. 3 & up. Also, **2-in-1 Slide** ($70) comes with built-in sprinkler that sprays kids as they zip down. Slide gets very fast when wet. 2–6. (800) 321-0183. Our testers also loved **Funnoodles' Giggle Wiggle Sprinkler** (Kidpower $10). The water flows through the soft foam tubing, making the tubes wiggle, and our testers certainly did giggle—loving the unpredictability of the water spray. 3 & up. (800) 545-7529.

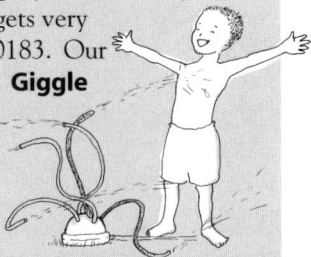

Wheel Toys—Trikes and Other Vehicles

Preschoolers will still use many of the vehicles featured in the Toddlers section. Vehicles such as the **Kiddie Coop, Fire Engine for Two,** *or* **Pickup Truck** *with no pedals remain solid favorites. Older preschoolers are also ready for tricycles and kiddie cars with pedals. The battery-operated vehicles that go 5 mph look tempting, but they won't do anything for big-muscle action. Here's what to look for in a three-wheel drive with pedal action:*

- Bigger is not better. Don't look for a trike to grow into.

- Take your child to the store to test drive and find the right size trike. Kids should be able to get on and off without assistance.

- Preschoolers need the security of a three-wheeler, which is more stable than a two-wheeler.

- A primary-colored bike can be reused by younger sibs regardless of their gender.

- See Safety Guidelines section for new safety standards for helmets.

Top-Rated Wheel Toys

Every year we test some of the newest wheeled toys—both trikes and four-wheelers. Our "ride-off" testers ranged in sizes and ages from 3 to 7. One common problem that affects the ride-ability of far too many vehicles remains the absence of treads. Kids are frustrated with plastic wheels that tend to spin without going anywhere.

■ Kettrike Happy 🏆

(Kettler $129.90) Gender-proof primary-colored trike with detachable push bar for adult. High back seat for added security. Designed for small 3s. Adult testers like the innovative control feature in the front wheel—an optional push/pull safety hub that adjusts for fixed drive or automatic coaster freewheeling. The **Jumbo** is slightly larger, and now multi-colored for '99. (804) 427-2400. Note: Neither Playskool nor Fisher-Price's less costly push bar trikes tested well. Playskool's had neither pedals nor room for foot-to-the-floor power.

Fisher-Price's was unnecessarily difficult to assemble.

■ Tough Trike 🏆

(Fisher-Price $29.99) This blue and yellow sporty trike with under-seat storage is well sized, sturdy, but lightweight. A good value! 3–5. (800) 432-5437.

■ Turbo Banking Jet

(Little Tikes $60) Amazing front wheel traction and side-to-side banking action thrilled young drivers of this pedal powered "jet." Steering comes naturally by controlling the joysticks on either side. An adjustable seat back extends the jet's play life. Since jet is low to the ground you may want to add a flag for attention and set firm boundaries. If you can get this built in the store, do it! One tester spent hours putting it together! 3–7 (800) 321-0183.

Four-Wheel Drives

■ Fire Engine for Two 🏆 PLATINUM AWARD

(Step 2 $40) Our testers loved the flashing lights and sounds of this bright red Fire Engine that has a rear seat for an extra firefighter. Runs on foot power sans pedals and is scaled for smaller kids from 2–4. For a larger kid, consider the new **Farm Tractor** ($30) or this company's really large **Big Rig** ($110). These are both pedal driven. (800) 347-8372.

■ Pickup Truck 🏆

(Little Tikes $69.99) Kids will get great pretend mileage from this yellow pickup truck. Flatbed has a drop-down tailgate equipped with hardhat and tool kit for emergency repairs. Runs on foot power for developing muscles and has a working steering wheel with horn. Big 2s–5. (800) 321-0183.

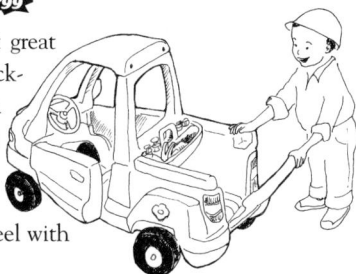

■ Sports Utility for Two

(Little Tikes $90) Testers loved this wide-bodied vehicle that's big enough for two kids to ride in together side by side. It runs on foot power (no pedals) so kids need to use big muscles for physical play. We like the gender-free sport-red color that makes this a vehicle that can be passed along to younger brothers or sisters. 2–5.

> 🛍 **SHOPPING TIP: Little Tikes suggests using a little liquid detergent on the connecting pieces of their toys if you are having difficulty putting them together.**

Stand-Alone Climbers

■ Little Tikes Playground

(Little Tikes $450) This top-of-the-line climber is part playhouse, part climber. It does not provide the kind of big-muscle climbing, dangling and jumping that classic monkey bars do, but kids had no complaints. They loved the multiple play areas with mini-tunnel, slides and platforms for imaginative play. Expensive but a solid investment. 3 & up. Platinum Award '95. For a small climber, we recommend the Blue Chip **Activity Gym** (Little Tikes $170) A durable climber with four colorful panels that lock together to form an all-purpose play environment. Has dominated the market for years because of its sturdiness. 3 & up. (800) 321-0183.

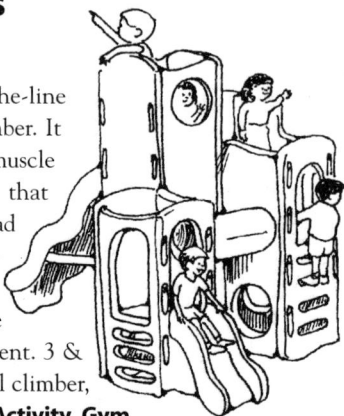

Playhouses

This is the ultimate toy for pretend play that will be used for several years of solo as well as social play. Kids as young as two love the magic of going in and out of a space that's scaled to child size. Threes and up are thrilled with the "privacy" of a little house of their own, and kids as old as six and seven will use it for all sorts of pretend.

Top-Rated Houses

There are a variety of playhouses to fit different tastes and budgets.

New and noteworthy this year is Step 2's gender-free **Red Barn** ($225) complete with double Dutch doors, silo, and working shutters. It has no built-in kitchen, which may be something you want, but it does have a table with two "milk can" seats for sit-down craft or snack times. Little Tikes' **Smallest Playhouse,** 46"H ($140), will be outgrown before the 52"H pastel **Country Cottage** ($200). For still grander, larger, and thematic housing, consider the 59"H **Log Cabin** ($250) or **Castle** ($250), or a huge **Victorian Mansion** ($400) that's 5' high and opens on one side. Step 2's **Drive-in Playhouse** ($160) comes with double-door opening for ride-in cars. Also from Step 2, **Welcome Home Playhouse** ($400) with a skylight! Scaled for kids as old as 10. (800) 347-8372. If you prefer a wooden structure and price is no object, you'll do best at a roadside fence dealer who also sells prefab sheds.

> **FREEBIE:** For temporary indoor housing, don't overlook the charm of a big cardboard box with cut-out windows and door or a tablecloth draped over a table for little campers to use as a tent. A great way to overcome rainy-day cabin fever.

Art Supplies

Markers, crayons, chalk, clay, and paint provide different experiences, all of which invite kids to express ideas and feelings, explore color and shapes, and develop muscles and control needed for writing and imagination. A supply of basics should include:

- Big crayons
- Washable markers
- Glue stick
- Safety scissors
- Finger-paint
- Colored construction paper
- Tempera paint
- Plain paper
- Molding material such as Play-Doh or plasticine

> **SHOPPING TIP:** Our testers were disappointed with fancy-shaped crayons that give less colorful

results than regular wax crayons. Preschoolers' little
hands also have better control with fatter crayons than
with the standard size.

Paints and Brushes

*Tempera paint is ideal for young children
because of its thick, opaque quality.
Watercolors are more appropriate for school-
aged children. Young children will have more
success with thick brushes than skinny
ones, which are harder to control. To
reduce the number of spills, invest in
paint containers sold with lids and openings just
wide enough for a thick paintbrush. Buying paint in
pint-sized squeeze bottles is more economical than buying small jars
of paint that will dry out. Look for both nontoxic and washable
labels on any art supplies you buy.*

■ Clay Model Maker Kit

(Alex $17) An open-ended kit that comes with both colorful model-
ing clay and air-hardening clay, as well as a roller, clay cutters, and
paints. 4 & up. (800) 666-2539.

■ Creative Art Starters

(Little Tikes $8) Preschool testers liked both the **MaskMania Project
Kit** and **Sweetheart Keeper'n'Jewels** sets. The latter includes materials for making necklaces with wooden buttons, beads, and paper,
plus a heart-shaped box to decorate and store jewels in. (800) 321-
0183.

■ Preschool Collage, Clay, & Puppets Kits

(Creativity for Kids $16 each)
While most craft kits are designed
for older kids and are end-prod-
uct-minded, these kits provide
enough open-ended materials to
give preschoolers an opportunity
to explore collaging, clay, or mak-
ing puppets. Develops kids' dexterity, creative thinking skills, and
imagination. 3s & up. (800) 642-2288.

■ **Sponge a Story** 🌟

(Alex $15) Comes with 12 big sponge shapes, paint, crayons, paper plates, and 4 large "settings" to decorate. 4 & up.

Q ACTIVITY TIP: Painting with straws is a great outdoor game. Take a large piece of construction paper and pour puddles of tempera paint on the paper. Preschoolers love blowing the paint with a straw to create their own designs.

■ **Magna Doodle** 🌟

(Fisher-Price $10 & up) An updated version of a classic with new magnetic drawing shapes that stay in place better. Kids and parents love this no-mess magnetic drawing board for home or on the go. Kids draw directly on the board with stylus or magnetic shapes. 3 & up. (800) 432-5437.

Q ACTIVITY TIP: Magic Painting is great fun. Have child draw on paper with a piece of wax or a white crayon. Then water down a bit of tempera and have child paint over invisible drawing. Abracadabra! The drawing appears!

Easels

Some say a flat table makes painting easier since the colors won't run. However, having an easel set up makes art materials accessible whenever the mood moves young artists.

Wooden Easels

■ **Tabletop Easel**

(Alex $40) If floor space is tight, consider a sturdy dual-sided tabletop hardwood easel with four-place paint-cup holder, 16" x 18" erase-board and painting surface, and a green chalkboard with ledge for erasers on the reverse side. Folds flat for convenient storage. 3 & up. Platinum Award '98. (800) 666-2539. For a traditional floor model, testers gave high ratings to those with chalkboards on one-side and write-and-wipe marker boards on the other (Back to Basics $89.95 & up). We suggest using big clips to hold paper rather than rollers, which our kid testers couldn't resist pulling to create a real paper trail! Item #998. (800) 356-5360.

Plastic Easels 🌟

Depending on your space and needs the following are top-rated choices: **Double Easel** *(Little Tikes $60) This bright red easel has a chalkboard on one side and a large clip that holds a pad of 17" x 20" paper. New for '99:* **9-in-1 Easy Adjust Easel** 🌟 **PLATINUM AWARD** *(Little Tikes $25). Takes little space and adjusts to nine different heights for tots to preteens (as shown). 3 & up. (800) 321-0183. If room permits, look at* **Creative Art Center** *(Step 2 $50). This art center has two easels and a worktable in between. 2 & up. (800) 347-8372. An innovative* **2-in-1 Easel Table** *(Fisher-Price $60) converts from a big table to a two-sided easel for chalk and painting. You need plenty of space for this one. Platinum Award '98. (800) 432-5437.*

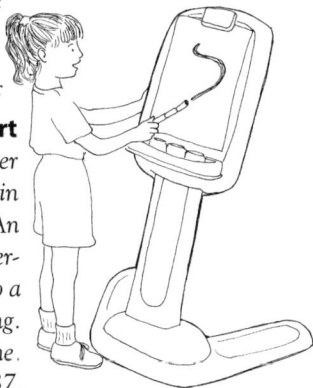

> **Q** ACTIVITY TIP: Take the 9-in-1 Easel outdoors. We sometimes forget how pleasant it is to paint out-doors and without the usual worries of getting paint on the floor.

🛍 Comparison Shopper— Laptop Easels

Fisher-Price wins hands down. Their **3-in-1 Portable Art Studio** (Platinum Award '98) (Fisher-Price $14.99) is slightly

bigger yet less expensive than Little Tikes' **Super Storage Travel Desk** and better designed with easy access supply drawers that swing out on either side. 3 & up. (800) 432-5437. For an even bigger floor-sitting model, our testers loved the **Creative Activities Floor Studio** (Little Tikes $30) for both projects and snack time! Comes with storage bins and an easel. 3 & up. (800) 321-0183.

Modeling Materials

■ Plasticine

(Alex / Crayola, $5 & up) This oil-based modeling material is what your old "clay" set probably contained. Unlike Play-Doh or clay, plasticine never hardens, though you may need to soften it up by kneading it before your child can work with it. It can be used again and again.

■ Play-Doh

(Hasbro $2 & up) This classic dough is still a favorite. We prefer the dough without the doodads since most of the kits are less open-ended and tough to do. This self-hardening material is still a favorite, but it dries out if left uncovered. 3 & up. (800) 752-9755.

> **FREEBIE: Cookie cutters, rolling pins, baby bottle rings, and other items around your kitchen make great tools for molding.**

■ Self-Hardening Clay

(Adica Pongo / Alex $3 & up) Kids can model with this material that dries in the air. It is more responsive to the touch than either Play-Doh or plasticine. Kids will need to learn to use water whenever they join one piece with another. Creations can be painted when clay dries. Found in toy and art supply shops.

Music and Movement

■ Follow-the-Lights Keyboard

(Mattel $30) Kids can play this Mickey Mouse keyboard three ways: Auto play has eight tunes, keyboard plays like a piano, or follow-the-lights mode that guides kids to eight preprogrammed songs. Has a loud or soft control, but be forewarned, this is a toy that you will hear—a lot. (800) 524-8697.

■ **Lollipop Drum**

(Woodstock Percussion $22) Preschoolers can easily hold onto the handle of this lollipop-shaped drum. Makes a pleasing sound according to both kid and parent testers. (800) 435-8863.

■ **Clatter Pillar** 🌟

(Small World $13) Hold the two ends of this "instrument" in your hands and as the plastic slats clatter and wiggle from side to side they make a great sound. Fun for rhythm bands or dancing along to any music. 3 & up. Also, top-rated, **RainBoMaker** ($17), a see-through plastic "rainstick" with colorful beads that makes a soothing sound. Or shake it for a maraca-like sound. 3 & up. (310) 645-9680.

■ **Song Magic Banjo** 🌟 PLATINUM AWARD

(Playskool $29.99) An innovative use of motion activation in this stringless banjo with Barney motif. Activated when player waves a hand in the center of the banjo. Plays 8 instruments and 8 songs, including "I Love You..." Comes with 3 AA batteries. 2–5. (800) 752-9755.

> **Q** ACTIVITY TIP: Use drum to beat out someone's first name. For example, Sa-man-tha would get three beats. Take turns guessing whose name is being clanged.

Preschool Furniture Basics

Table and Chairs

These are convenient pieces of basic gear that will be used for artwork, puzzles, tea parties, and even lunch. You'll find many choices in both plastic and wood. This is a decorating choice as well as a functional one. For safety and buying checklist, see page 48 in the Toddlers chapter.

Best Travel Toys

Preschoolers can entertain themselves for short periods of time with toys and art supplies. A well-loved soft doll or mini-setting with multiple pieces makes for a cozy pretend play. At this stage, a piece of home whether it's a toy or blanket is still important. One of the best ways to make time fly is to bring along a tape player with favorite songs or stories to enjoy. For restaurant stops, pack a plastic baggie filled with simple games, cards, or crayons and paper to fill time before the breadbasket arrives. Bring along a handful of paperbacks (instead of hardcovers) to share and for independent "reading." Here are some of our favorites:

Top-rated take-alongs

■ Baby Nurse Doll Car Seat/Carrier

(Berchet $25.95) Perfect for dolls on the go, this cotton car seat has a safety harness just like the real thing, and converts to a backpack. Fits an 8"–16" doll or stuffed animal. 3 & up. (800) 445-8347.

■ Feltkids Playsets 🌟⁹⁹

(Learning Curve $9.99 & up) These felt cutouts are ideal for language development, pretending, and storytelling. They will also keep children occupied in the back seat. **The Travel Playset** ($29.99) has vehicles, bridge, people, and camp site in a 14" x 11" case with handles that opens to a generous felt surface. Top-rated sets for '99: **Fairyland, Glow-in-the-Dark Space Adventure, Pony Play; Madeline's Garden** and **Blue's Clues.** 3 & up. (800) 704-8697.

■ 3-in-1 Portable Art Studio (see laptop easels)

■ Magic Cloth Paper Dolls 🌟⁹⁹

(Schylling $12) Adorable cutout magnetic dolls and familiar characters (such as Mr. Potato Head, Arthur, Big Bird) with outfits, and a play board. New sets for '99 include Arthur's sister, **D.W., Rugrats,** and **Blue's Clues.** 3 & up. (800) 541-2929.

■ **Monstrous Vumpets & Spunky Monkeys** 99

(Manhattan Toy $5 each) These floppy beanbag velour pets are the tamest monsters & most playful monkeys we've ever found. Perfect little handfuls for back seat players. 4 & up. (800) 474-2454.

■ **Three Bears House** 99

(Pockets of Learning $35) Every child's favorite tale comes to life with this little zip-and-carry fabric house. Fitted out with fabric bears, Goldilocks, and, of course, chairs and beds that are too hard, too soft, and just right. Perfect for retelling the original and making up your own adventures. Also from the same maker, a charming **Zip and Carry Farm** ($35). 2 1/2 & up. (800) 635-2994.

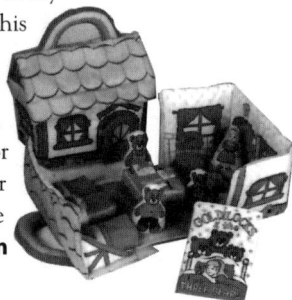

■ **Travel Magna Doodle**

(Fisher-Price $10 & up) This no-mess magnetic drawing tool with tied-on "pen" is perfect for drawing, tic-tac-toe, and even writing letters and numbers. (800) 432-5437.

Best Third and Fourth Birthday Gifts for Every Budget

Big Ticket ($100 Plus)	**Red Barn** (Step 2) or set of wooden blocks
$100 & under	**Wooden Train** set or **Shop & Cook Kitchen** (Fisher-Price) or **Actimates Barney** (Microsoft)
Under $50	**Fire Engine For Two** (Step 2) or **Talking Playtime Big Bird** (Tyco) or **Tabletop Puppet Theatre** or **Easel** (Alex)

Under $25   **Tournament Golf Set** (Little Tikes) or
Lollipop Drum (Woodstock Percussion) or
Arthur/D.W. Dolls (Eden or Playskool)

Under $20   **Lego Duplo Playtable** (Lego) or
Busytown Board Game (Ravensburger)

Under $15   **3-in-1 Portable Art Studio** (Fisher-Price)
or **Musical Cake Surprise** (Fisher-Price) or
Preschool Collage & Puppet Kits
(Creativity for Kids)

Under $10   **Monstrous Vumpets or Spunky Monkeys**
(Manhattan Toy) or **Nobbie Gertie Ball**
(Small World)

4 • Early School Years
Five to Ten Years

What to Expect Developmentally

Learning Through Play. During the early school years, as children begin their formal education, play continues to be an important path to learning. Now more complex games, puzzles, and toys offer kids satisfying ways to practice and reinforce the new skills they are acquiring in the classroom.

Dexterity and Problem-Solving Ability. School-aged kids have the dexterity to handle more elaborate building toys and art materials. They are curious about how things work and take pride in making things that can be used for play or displayed with pride.

Active Group Play. These early school years are a very social time when kids long for acceptance among their peers. Bikes and sporting equipment take on new importance as the social ticket to being one of the kids. Children try their hand at more formal team sports where being an able player is a way of belonging.

Independent Discovery. Although these are years when happiness is being with a friend, children also enjoy and benefit from solo time. Many of the products selected here are good tools for such self-sufficient and satisfying skills.

 BASIC GEAR CHECKLIST FOR EARLY SCHOOL AGE

✓ Sports equipment
✓ Craft kits
✓ Musical instruments
✓ Water paints, markers, stampers
✓ Two-wheeler with training wheels
✓ Lego and other construction sets
✓ Electronic game/learning machines

✓ Dolls/soft animals
✓ Board games
✓ Tape player and tapes

 Toys to Avoid

These toys pose safety hazards:

✓ Chemistry sets that can cause serious accidents
✓ Plug-in toys that heat up with light bulbs and can give kids serious burns
✓ Audio equipment with volume controls that cannot be locked
✓ Projectile toys such as darts, rockets, B-B guns, or other toys with flying parts that can do serious damage
✓ Super-powered water guns that can cause abrasions
✓ Toys with small parts if there are young children in the house

The following is developmentally inappropriate:

✓ An abundance of toys that reinforce gender stereotypes; for example, hair play for girls and gun play for boys

Pretend Play

School-age kids have not outgrown the joys of pretending. They like elaborate and realistic props for stepping into the roles of storekeeper, athlete, or race car driver. For some, mini-settings such as puppet theaters, doll houses, and castles are a preferable route to make-believe. This is also the age when collecting miniature vehicles and action figures can become a passion. Such figures generally reflect the latest cartoon or movie feature. Nobody needs all the pieces, although many

kids want them all. At this stage, owning a few pieces of the hottest "in" character represents a way of belonging.

Puppets and Puppet Stages

Puppets provide an excellent way for kids to develop language and storytelling skills that are the underpinning for reading and writing. Many of the puppets and stages in the Preschool section will get lots of mileage now. Older kids may also become interested in making shadow, stick, or hand puppets of their own.

■ Finger Puppet Theater 🏅 PLATINUM AWARD

(Manhattan Toy $30) This wonderful new fabric stage has a working curtain and a foldout platform on which finger puppets can perform. Folds up for easy portability and has storage space for several puppets. 4 & up. (800) 747-2454.

■ Finger Puppets 🏅

You'll find an amazing variety of finger puppets to inspire quiet fantasy play and story telling. Some of the best for 🏅: **Stylin' Steppers** 🏅 (Manhattan Toy $5 each) Whimsical people-like rabbits, frogs, cows, and ducks are ready to take a stylish stroll. Or for jungle tales choose a lion, monkey, zebra, elephant, and giraffe. For more realistic critters: **Woofers, Finger Fillies, & Farmerellas.** (800) 747-2454. **Curious George** (Gund $7). (732) 248-1500; **Tippy Toes** (Mary Meyer $5 & up) work on the two-fingers-do-the-walking principle. We like the astronaut, cowboy, or storybook collections. 4 & up. (800) 451-4387.

■ Community Street or Medieval Castle Theater 🏅

(Creative Education of Canada $25 each) These cardboard tabletop theaters are surprisingly sturdy, have a curtain, and come with three felt hand puppets that match the themes. 4 & up. (800) 982-2642.

Favorite Hand Puppets

■ Emergency Rescue Squad Puppets
BLUE CHIP

(Learning Resources $19.95 set of 4) Multicultural

workers—doctor, paramedic, police officer, and firefighter with vinyl heads and cloth bodies. 4 & up. (800) 222-3909.

■ **Lacing Puppets** 🌟

(Lauri $8 & up) Choose from a variety of precut felt puppet sets with different themes that kids lace together and then use. Choose pre-cut Bunnies, Bugs, or People puppets. Kits come with yarn and big plastic needle for sewing (which develops fine motor skills kids need for writing). New for 🌟, **Swamp Puppets** ($11.95). (800) 451-0520.

■ **Polar Bear** 🌟

(Folkmanis $22) Realistic full-bodied polar bear is ready for Arctic action. See this company's line of amazing winged and furry creatures. 5 & up. (800) 443-4463.

■ **Spellcasters**

(Manhattan Toy $10 each) A wizard, dragon, and unicorn with licks of gold and silver on velour will cast their spells and combine with **Royal Puppets** (see preschool). Five-finger control makes for very animated story telling. 6 & up. (800) 747-2454.

Dollhouses and Other Pretend Environments and Props

Kids are ready now for finer details in house and furnishings. Specialty dollhouse shops and crafts stores sell prefabs and custom houses to fit all budgets. The play settings recommended here require construction skills and adult involvement.

■ **Victorian Doll House** BLUE CHIP

(Playmobil $199 & up) Don't try to set this up before you give it! Putting it together is part of the fun. A challenging but well-designed model to construct together. When the deed is done, it will be used for dramatic play. 6 & up. Platinum Award '95. (800) 752-9662.

■ Castles

A handsome 114-piece wood **Castle** (Small World $50) can be combined with blocks or used for open-ended build-and-play fun. Blocks with pegs fit together and come with turrets, drawbridge, and knights. Says 3 & up, we'd say 5–7s. (310) 645-9680. For older builders, consider Lego's **Night Lords' Castle** (Lego $80) with trap doors, dragon, and other spooks. 8–12. (800) 233-8756 .

■ Polar Command 🌟99

(Galoob $14.95) If you have a reluctant bather this might help. One of a series of mini-settings with detailed mini-boats, sea planes, wildlife, radar instruments and research station that floats! Also special, **Sea Squall Station.** 5 & up.

Props for Pretend

See Preschool chapter for this year's best costumes.

■ Let's Pretend Restaurant

(Creativity for Kids $17) Want to open a restaurant? Here's a kit with a cook's hat, order pad, menus, signs, a checked table cloth, money, and fake food. We still love the classic **Paraphernalia for Pretending Kit** ($17) with gear for restaurant as well as theater, stores, and offices. 4 & up. (800) 642-2288.

■ Pretend & Play Calculator Cash Register

(Learning Resources $39.95) A solar-powered register with working calculator and digital display, comes loaded with play money and a credit card. Expensive but better made than any other. A marvelous tool with pretend and math skills built into the action. Marked 4 & up, but a solid choice for school-aged kids who are learning to use a calculator. (800) 222-3909.

■ Kitty Vet Kit 🌟99

(Battat $28) For vets in the making, this kit has far more detailed props than Little Tikes for setting up an office and curing ailing pets—not to mention a plush kitten. 5 & up. (800) 247-6144.

Dolls

Now's the time when girls often get heavily invested in dolls with tons of paraphernalia. Although five- and six-year-old boys often find ways to play with a cousin's or sister's doll or dollhouse, they are more likely to choose action figures for this kind of play. Both boys and girls continue to enjoy soft stuffed animals, the zanier the better.

For many years, the only kinds of dolls around were blonde with blue eyes but, happily, more manufacturers today are creating dolls that reflect our cultural diversity. Here are some of the best:

■ American Girl and American Girl of Today

(Pleasant Co. $82) This mail-order-only company has made its name with exquisite dolls from different periods in American history. There are books for each doll—a wonderful way to introduce history to kids. Last year's Platinum Award winner, **Josefina** is the newest from the historic line. She is an 18" Hispanic girl growing up in New Mexico in 1824. The American Girl of Today collection allows you to choose one of 20 contemporary-looking dolls with Caucasian, African-American, Hispanic, and Asian-American skin tones and features. Each comes with a journal for writing. Platinum Award '96. 6 & up. (800) 845-0005.

■ Global Friends Collection

(Global Friends $59 & up) Mariko of Japan, Mei Ling of China, and Clio of France are just three of the stunning foreign dolls in this collection that also has books, clothing, furniture, and outstanding videos. Global Friends introduce kids to contemporary girls of other cultures. Videos of Mariko and Clio show kids at school and at home, and celebrating holidays. (One Japanese-American family did note that some of the details were off, i.e., rice paper is not made of rice and tea sets in Japan do not come with sugar bowls and creamers.) There are African, South American, English, German, & Egyptian dolls plus a newsletter and pen pal clubs. Mail-order only. 6 & up. (800) 393-5421.

■ Jamaica

(Olmec $34.99) Jamaica, an 18" African-American beauty, has glorious hair and accessories to make cornrows and other hairstyles. She wears a dress of Kente fabric. 5 & up. For the fashion doll set look for Amani, an African-American princess. (800) 677-6966.

■ International Collection

(Madame Alexander $50 each) These 8" dolls wear authentic costumes from other lands. Leaving them on display will be difficult for all but the oldest girls in this group. 8 & up. (212) 283-5900.

Other Notable Dolls

■ Barbie UPDATE 💀

(Mattel $15 & up) Barbie is very sports-minded this year. Our testers loved the spinning Olympic Skating Barbie and Ken ($30). We are also delighted that Barbie has joined the WNBA ($19.99) and will be fit, active, and going to the boards. Ken has a new career this year; he's a doctor. ($15.99) (800) 524-8697.

■ Les Mini Corolline 💀 PLATINUM AWARD

(Corolle $20 each) You won't know which to pick from this group of 8" blonde and brunette dolls. Each comes with two outfits. We love the schoolgirl with pleated skirt, backpack, and plaid smock; or the ballerina with tutu plus leotard and leg warmers; a rider with English and Western riding clothes; and a hiker with straw hat and sleeping cot. Amazing furniture such as a bed, table and chair set, or armoire ($25 each) are scaled to size and beautifully finished in white. Also very special, **Corolline** 💀 ($50), an 11" beauty who comes with a small china tea set. Ooh-la-la! 4–8. (800) 628-3655.

■ Muffy VanderBear and Hoppy VanderHare
💀 PLATINUM AWARD

(North American Bear Co. $20 each) These long-time favorites of ours have outdone themselves this year with an exquisite blue & white **Pagoda Collection** 💀 (PLATINUM AWARD). Accessories include a tea-set with both char-

acters printed on the fabric and china. Also charming, **Sleddin'** and **Skeddadlin'** set in winter gear. Both 7" tall with articulated arms and legs. Also new, **Muffy Starter Set** ($29.95) comes with Muffy in her underwear, a signature dress and shoes—a great value! 6 & up. (800) 682-3427.

Electric Train Sets

Many train buffs will tell you that this is the stage when their romance with trains began.

Shopping Tips

▥ Select HO gauge for beginners. Smaller trains and tracks can be frustrating and tricky to put together. Larger-gauge sets take up a tremendous amount of space, so you generally end up with just a boring circle of track.

▥ Start with a basic set and enough track to make an interesting roadbed.

▥ Since trains are plug-in electrical items, they are labeled for 8 & up. Younger children may enjoy them, but they should be used only with adult supervision.

Racing Car and Track Sets

Over the years, our testers have been disappointed with the perfor-mance of most racing car sets. "This looked great on TV, but we can't keep the cars on the track," or, "Is this all it does?" Most kids want more options. These sets delivered as promised: **Hot Wheels Starter Set** *(Mattel $17) is a super-fast motorized cloverleaf track. For best results tape down the track. (800) 524-8697. Best of the lot:*

■ **X-V Racers Cyclone** ⭐ **PLATINUM AWARD**

(Mattel $20) Last year we rated the **Triple Loop Set** the best track set we've tested in years (Platinum Award '98). **The Cyclone,** with tighter triple loops, also delivers. Use the power charger to rev up one specially motorized Hot Wheels car and your car will zoom around the track.

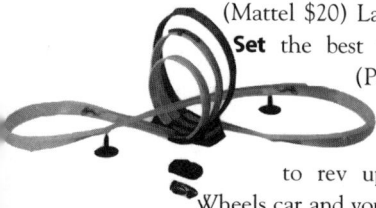

An extra car is a must even though it's an additional $10! Also new for
🌟 **Off Road X-V Racers.** 5 & up. (800) 524-TOYS.

■ Rokenbok Expandable RC Building System
🌟 PLATINUM AWARD

(Rokenbok $149 & up) Forget about
those big racing car set-ups, this
does more than just racing in circles! This innovative system is
expensive, but it is also more open-ended,
expandable, and offers greater interest and challenge than any
train/car set we've ever seen. The **Basic Start** set has 152 pieces, one
dump truck, a ball run and command deck for loading and running
vehicles up and down the ramps. The **Deluxe Factory ($199)** has a
motorized conveyer. There are different vehicles but our testers liked
the dump truck best ("it gets to do more!"). 6 & up with adult assistance. Takes 3 AA batteries. Amazing! (888) 476-5265.

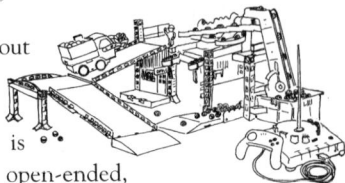

Trucks and Cars

■ Tyco R/C Psycho 🌟

(Mattel $54.99) The latest radio control vehicle that twists and flips
with oversized back wheels. Takes practice! Still recommended,
Turbo Tantrum 6.0V. 7 & up. (800) 524-8697.

■ Tyco Revolver RC Stunt Vehicle 🌟 PLATINUM AWARD

(Mattel $30) Smaller-scaled than last season's Tantrum R.C., this
vehicle does gyro stunts, flips in circles, does 360-degree wheelies,
and runs with blazing speed. Easier to operate than larger vehicles.
Takes 4 AA batteries and a 9 volt which are not included. Does not
have a rechargeable pack. 5 & up. (800) 367-8926.

■ Sound Machine Water Cannon   BLUE CHIP

(Nylint $46) The ultimate fire engine, with electronic sounds repro-
duced from a real fire truck—including air brakes, warning signals,
and sirens. Has flashing lights and a 35" boom that pivots. 5 & up.
Platinum Award '94. (800) 397-8697.

Construction Toys

What kids learn from
construction toys

Builders learn to follow directions and

develop dexterity, problem-solving skills, and stick-to-itiveness. Success is not always instant. Updated classics such as **Lincoln Logs** *and* **Tinkertoys** *(Hasbro), are more appropriate for this age even though they are labeled for preschoolers.* **Glueless Snap Models** *(Ertl) are also a good place to start for beginning model builders.*

What you should know before you buy:

    As their dexterity develops, kids can handle small-er pieces and more complex building sets.

    Provide a variety of building sets rather than just one type because building with Legos, K'nex, and Erector Sets involves different, but equally valuable, skills.

    Start with open-ended sets that can be built in mul-tiple ways. As your child becomes a more confident builder, move on to small models.

    Age labels on most building sets are not accurate. If the box says 5 & up and your 5-year-old needs a lot of assistance—the problem is with the label and not your child.

    On the plus side, working on one of these sets together can be rewarding. Be careful not to take over; break the project into do-able parts to build confi-dence.

    Keep in mind that less can be more. Start with do-able sets in the $15–$20 range that help your child to learn the particular building strategies.

    Girls as well as boys need to develop spatial/visual skills that are built into construction toys.

Top-Rated Open-Ended Construction Sets

■ **Lego Free-Style Basic Building Sets** BLUE CHIP

(Lego $1.99–$44.99) The granddaddy of plastic building blocks, Legos are a must-have for this age group. New sets include a mix of bricks, wheels, doors, and mini-figures. Also a great value, **Lego Freestyle Playtable** ✿ ($15) comes with 300+ pieces. 5–7. (800) 233-8756.

■ **Toobers & Zots** 🌟

(HandsOn Toys $5 & up) An innovative bendable foam shapes set, '96 Platinum Award winner remains a hit with testers who liked the **Kit & Kabooble Set** ($49.95) with large ball and cube shapes called "Oobles" and two-sided/two-colored "flip-flop" zots. New for 🌟, **Flower** and **Dino** sets. 5 & up. (781) 932-8774.

■ **Zolo** 🌟

(Wild Planet $15 & up) An abstract and open-ended creative building set with endless constructions children can build. Works on the same principle as your old Tinkertoys, with post-and-hole pieces. Done in plastic, in Memphis-style colors and shapes. Testers wished that the new motorized kit, **Moto Zolo,** had more pieces that were activated by the motor. Also new for 🌟, **Miniature Zolo** looked promising, but was not ready for testing. (800) 247-6570.

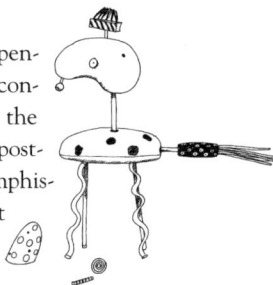

Theme and Pattern Construction Sets

■ **Lego Play Systems** 🌟

(Lego $15 & up) Our testers gave these top-ratings: **Hydro Search Sub** for underwater adventures ($49.99/289 pieces) and **Stingray Stormer** ($69.99/252 pieces) comes with secret compartments, escape pods, and crew of divers. 8–12. For builders who like settings, **Extreme Team Challenge** ($49.99/354 pieces) comes with a play setting, a monster truck, raft, bridge, and mountain. Older builders rated **Celestial Stinger** the **PLATINUM AWARD** winner 🌟 ($49.99/398 pieces.) 8 & up. It comes with flashing lights and eerie sounds. Remember to start with smaller sets for serious builders-in-training: a good set is **Whirling Time Warper** ($19.99/147 pieces). 7 & up. (800) 233-8756. See Computer Chapter for **Lego Mindstorm.**

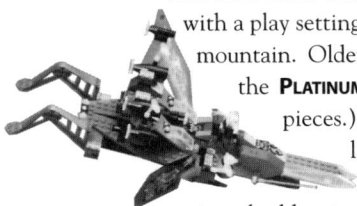

Top-Rated Motorized Sets

■ **Chaos** 🌟

(Chaos $135) In answer to our question, "What did your child like about this toy?" the answer was, "EVERYTHING!" Both boys and girls testing this amazing construction set loved the immense Rube-

Goldberg-like inventions they built. A playful way to give kids a hands-on experience with basic science and engineering principles, problem solving, spatial relationships, and creative thinking. Adult help needed. New for ➣99✦ : smaller starter and intermediate kits. 10 & up. Platinum Award '98. (314) 567-9097.

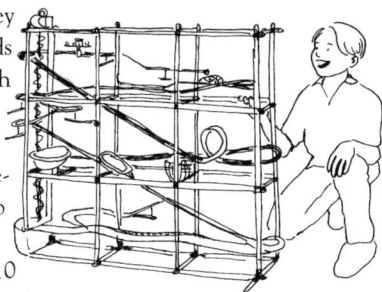

■ Erector Playsystem and Erector ➣99✦

(Irwin $20 & up) For beginners, stick with Erector Playsystem plastic models, such as last year's Platinum Award-winning **Desert Raider** ($29.99) which makes three different models with pull back friction motors. Testers liked playing with their vehicles almost as much as building them. Also top-rated, **Rugged Rig** set ($50). 6–8. For older builders, classic metal building sets are still challenging. Look at sets: **Evolution 2** and **3** both come with battery-operated motors and enough pieces so kids can build a variety of models. (800) 268-1733.

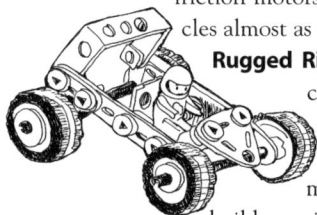

■ K'nex ➣99✦

(K'nex $14 & up) K'nex really took off when they started building kits with friction-, battery-, or solar-powered motors. Beginners should start with small friction motor sets. Testers report that you need more finger strength with K'nex than with Legos. Top-rated kits for ➣99✦ : **Solar Power 10 Model Stunt Kit** ($49.99) and **Lost Mines Power Tower Crane** ($99). Previous winners: **Solar Power K'nex 10 Model set, K'nexosaurus, Big Wheel Racers, and Bumper Cars.** 8 & up. (800) 54-5639.

■ Lego Technic ➣99✦

(Lego $10 & up) Designed to teach kids how gears, pulleys, wheels, and axles work, these are for experienced builders. Outstanding choices for ➣99✦ : **Mountain Rambler** ($29.99/244 pieces) and **Mud Masher** ($12.99/120 pieces). Previous winners: **Tred Trekker** ($20/186 pieces); **Search Sub** Platinum Award '98. ($44.99/376 pieces). For 10 & up. To power any model, use **Power Pack** ($36). (800) 233-8756.

■ Robotix 🎯

(Learning Curve $8 & up) Testers loved creating robots that move on RC command. Be forewarned: Pictorial instructions were hard to follow—even an 11-year-old needed help getting started, but soon could create new robots. Start with smaller sets such as **Arctic Glider** 🎯 . 7–12. (800) 704-8697.

Games

Classic and New Games

Now's the time when kids begin really to enjoy playing games with rules, both with friends and family. Of course, winning is still more fun than losing, and playing by the rules isn't always easy. That's the bad news. The good news is that many of the best board games are both entertaining and educational. Many games can improve math, spelling, memory, and reading skills in a more enjoyable way than the old flash card/extra workbook routine. Game playing also builds important cooperative social skills. For 5s & 6s, now's the time for classic Blue Chip games such as:

Parcheesi	**Dominoes**	**Chutes and Ladders**
Checkers	**Lotto**	**Trouble**
Uno	**Pick-up-Sticks**	**What's My Name?**
Connect 4		

For 7s, 8s, and up, try classics such as:

Othello	**Yahtzee**	**Monopoly Jr.**
Sorry	**Pictionary Jr.**	**Clue**
Chess	**Scrabble**	**Twister**
Upwords	**Bingo**	**Music Maestro II**
Boggle	**Life**	**Scattergories Junior**
Battleship	**Chinese Checkers**	**Quarto!**

■ Dog Dice and Wear'n'Tear

(Gamewright $10 each) Dog Dice is a clever twist on bingo that requires players to look for two attributes of four different dogs in order to place play bones on their board until someone yells "Hot Dog!" 6 & up. **Wear 'n' Tear** is a fast-

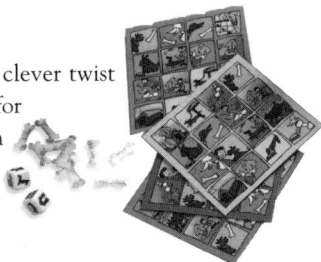

paced sequencing card game that's a bit like a classic game of War. Players must get rid of all their clothing cards in order from caps to shoes. No turn-taking here—it's a free-for-all! 6 & up. Platinum Award '98. (800) 638-7568.

■ I Spy Memory Game

(Briarpatch $19.95) Based on the popular book series, these 75 cards have matches that show pairs of objects, but often from another angle or in a different size or location. Can be played at varying levels of difficulty and enjoyed solo, one-on-one, or cooperatively. 4–8. Platinum Award '96. (800) 232-7427.

■ Knock Knock Mr. Potato Head 🏷99

(Playskool $24.99) If you have a knock-knock fan in your family, this interactive doll that tells 50 jokes randomly will be a hit. Pauses long enough for player to say, "Who's there?" and "___ who?" They say 3 & up, we say more like 5 & up to really get the jokes. Takes 3 AA batteries. (800) 852-9755.

■ Kuba 🏷99

(Patch Products $30) A handsome and challenging marble game where your object is to capture seven of the red marbles by pushing them off the board with your black or white marbles. Only problem: your opponent has the same mission. Easy to learn, fun to play, and develops flexible thinking, as well as strategy skills. (800) 524-4263. 10 & up.

■ Lingo Bingo 🏷99

(Learning Resources $15.95) Beginning readers can play rhyming word or beginning sound game with this variation on Bingo game. Games are short but reinforce phonic skills. 5 & up. Also recommended, **Python Path** ($12.95), a phonics game where kids land on a beginning sound and must make up a three or four letter word with the word endings on the dice thrown. 6 & up. (800) 222-3909.

■ Lite Brite Blue Chip

(Hasbro $14,99) This 30-year-old classic is still a great favorite for school aged kids. Requires fine motor skills, patience, and stickability as well as reading color codes, counting, following a pattern and developing the strategies for working one line or section or color at a time. Breaking the task into small do-able steps is something children need to learn when undertaking big tasks. Less open-ended than many toys, but comes with blanks for kids to make their own designs, too.

■ Round the Bend 99 PLATINUM AWARD

(International Playthings $20) In this twisting, turning game players build a pipeline from one side of the board to another. This is harder than it looks! Kids need strategy and the ability to see spatial relationships to translate from one-dimensional images to three-dimensional forms. 5 & up. (800) 445-8347.

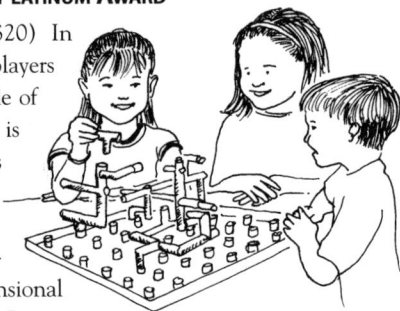

Math Games and Equipment

■ Aliens 99

(Gamewright $10) This card game is a variation on War with some extra math thrown in without spoiling the fun. Odd and Even Eater cards push kids to think of more than high and low numbers while remembering which cards are immune to space germs. Quick and entertaining. 7 & up. (800) 638-7568.

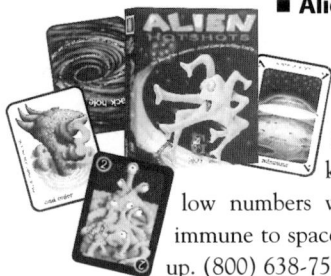

■ Mad Math 99

(Patrick Comm. $17.99) Knowing your multiplication tables is not required, but Mad Math provides a playful way to reinforce them. You play on a multiplication table so the answers are on the board. Kids not only learn to read the grid, they begin to see patterns. It's not like some dreaded "game" that's good for you—it's actually "edutaining." 9 & up. (888) 834-2380.

■ Pivot 99

(Wizards of the Coast $6.99) You have to keep track of both direction of play, which changes from clockwise to counterclockwise, and remember the card values of greater or less than—for 3 or more players. Play is in the luck of the draw rather than in serious strategy, but this is fun for mixed generations. Also fun, a color game, **Go Wild.**

Both good for travel. (425) 226-6500.

■ Rat-a-Tat Cat

(Gamewright $10) A fun card game that uses math concepts of greater and less than and challenges memory skills. The object is to get rid of the high cards (rats) and have the lowest hand with low scoring cats. 6 & up. Also top-rated, **Slamwich** and **Stone Soup.** 6 & up. Platinum Award '97. (800) 638-7568.

■ Sum Swamp 🌟99

(Learning Resources $12.95) An entertaining way to build speed and the ability to switch gears from adding to subtracting with simple math. Players toss three dice, one with plus or minus signs as they move their critter through the swamp where they sometimes have to deal with odds and evens. Right on the mark for late first, early second grade. Also top-rated, **Auntie Pasta's Fraction Game.** (800) 222-3909.

■ Timing it Right 🌟99

(Learning Resources $12.95) For kids who are beyond telling time by the hour or half hour, this board game challenges them to figure out time in more complex ways in order to win. Toss the "time" die and it directs you to move ahead by time, e.g., 1 hr 1/2, and then you must follow the directions of the time book to get your next move. Fun for reinforcing time skills. 7 & up. (800) 222-3909.

Money Concept Games

■ Bunny Money 🌟99

(International Playthings $20) If they know the storybook, they'll love this young math game. Like Max and Ruby, players have a shopping list and have to buy what's on their list before they run out of money. Younger than Monopoly Junior, this is a good one for parents and kids 5 & up. (800) 445-8347.

NOTABLE PREVIOUS WINNERS

Cool Cash Bingo (Learning Resources $17.95) A fast-paced pair of games for learning to add, subtract, and make small change with coins. 7 & up. **Moneywise Kids** (Aristoplay $15) Two games in one:

learning how to make change from $100 and learning how to pay your bills with $100 (not easy!). 7 & up. (888) 478-4263. Also, **Presto Change-O Game** (Educational Insights $24.95) This one deals in coins as well as dollars. (800) 933-3277.

Math Manipulatives

Concrete materials give kids a greater understanding of counting and calculating. Don't rush to take these materials away from kids. They help make the transition to abstract thinking easier.
Blue Chip choices are: **Math in a Bag** *(Water Street $25) Giant-sized cuisenaire rods. (800) 866-8228.* **Unifix Cubes** *(Didax $19.95) Beginning math students use these cubes for understanding early math concepts. (800) 433-4329.* **Primary Time Teacher Learning Clock Junior** *(Learning Resources $14.95) As kids move the minute hand, the synchronized and color-coded digital display also tells the time in 5-minute increments. (800) 222-3909.* **Tic-Tock Answer Clock** *(Tomy $11) Same principle as above but in the shape of an owl. (800) 445-8347.*

■ Pick-Up Stix

(Small World $3) We've tried plastic sticks and over-sized wooden ones, but these old fashioned wooden pick-up stix are "just right." You really can use the tips to tip and pick them up and color bands make them more valuable than most for score keeping—yellow bands = 50 points, red bands = 45, etc. Adding gets a work-out! This classic game also develops eye-hand coordination and fine motor skills, such as those needed for writing. Adjust value of stix to match child's math skills. 5 & up. (310) 645-9680.

Electronic Quiz Machines

Most math quiz machines are like electronic flash cards—good for drilling basics in addition, subtraction, multiplication, and division. Kids often prefer them to flashcards, since they can quiz themselves and work at their own speed. Be forewarned: On most electronic quiz toys, two-digit answers have to be answered with tens first.

This is contrary to the way kids are taught to do math, especially when regrouping is involved, so machines may be confusing. Many quiz machines also go too far and fast. Try them before you bring one home. Remember, machines can't clarify repeated mistakes but they can provide practice, speed, and reinforce what kids know.

Two good choices: **Number Wise** (Tiger $14.99) *Handheld game that works as both a calculator (good for checking homework) and quiz game machine. (847) 913-8100.* **Math Safari** *(Educational Insights $99.95) Machine uses quiz books with pictorial images so child has more to work with than abstract symbols & calculations. (800) 933-3277. For other top-rated choices, see p. 115.*

Puzzles and Brainteasers

Putting jigsaw puzzles and brainteasers together calls for visual perception, eye/hand coordination, patience, and problem-solving skills. During their early school years, kids should build from 25-piece puzzles to 50- and 100-plus pieces.

Beginners' Puzzles—Under 50 pieces

■ **A–Z Panels** BLUE CHIP ⭐

(Lauri $8.95) Not only does fitting the rubbery letters in and out of the puzzle frame help kids learn to know and name the letters, but handling the 3-D letters also gives kids a feel for their shapes. Updated this year with useful pictures under each letter. Also, **Kids Perception Puzzle** ($7.50), figures in slightly different poses that help kids look at small differences, just as they must when reading words that look almost alike, such as "cap" and "cup." 4–7. (800) 451-0520.

■ **Backyard Bugs**

(Frank Schaffer $14.95) Forty-eight big pieces and an identification key for learning the names of the bigger-than-life-sized bugs are found in this 5'-long beautiful garden scene. (800) 421-5565. Also, **Endangered Animals** (48 pieces become a 5'-long mural). 5 & up. (800) 421-5565.

■ **I Spy 1, 2, 3... Floor Puzzle** ⭐

(Briarpatch $14.95) Our testers loved working on this oversized 35-piece floor puzzle taken from the pages of *I Spy School Days*. After kids put together the puzzle, they have to locate the objects in the riddle. A good parent and child activity. Also top-rated, 63–100-piece puzzles in this series. (800) 232-7427.

■ **Mama Do You Love Me?** 🌟99

(Mudpuppy $12.95) With an illustration by Barbara Lavallee from Barbara Joosse's classic storybook, this is the newest in a line of picturebook puzzles from such books as *Madeline* and *Stellaluna*. (212) 354-8840.

■ **Parquetry Blocks and Cards** BLUE CHIP

(Learning Resources $26.95) Thirty-two geometric-shaped tiles are arranged on top of 20 colorful patterns. Advanced players can use tiles without the pattern. Develops skills in matching and sequencing patterns—skills that are needed in putting letters together to make words. 5–8. (800) 222-3909.

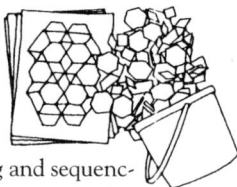

Intermediate—50+ Pieces and Shaped Puzzles

■ **Giraffes** 🌟99

(Frank Schaffer $14.95) Due to the pattern and lack of hard edges, this oversized 24-piece puzzle was a challenge for 5-year-old testers. Very satisfying. Also handsome, **Rainforest Frogs** ($14.95) 50-piece floor puzzle that turns into a 2' x 3' picture. Frogs are not whole pieces. Says 4 & up, but we'd say more like 5. (800) 421-5565.

■ **Endangered Species**

(Anything's Puzzable $17.95) One of an amazing collection of circular puzzles with whole creatures that fit together. Interesting facts appear on back of each puzzle piece. Testers also loved the 69-piece **World Beneath the Sea** and the 75-piece **World of Dinosaurs.** With adult help, 5 & up. Platinum Award '98. (800) 984-8486.

■ **Puzz-3-D** 🌟99

(Hasbro $10 & up) We liked these miniature three-dimensional puzzles with fewer pieces than the originals, but super-challenging. Try the **Empire State Building** or the **Eiffel Tower.**

NOTABLE PREVIOUS WINNERS

Secrets of the Pyramid (Great American Puzzle Factory $12) 60 pieces with mysterious treasures that magically appear when rubbed. Also fun, **Underwater Surprises.** Says 4 & up, but subject fits better for 6 & up. (800) 922-1194. **Arthur Goes to School** (Great American Puzzle Factory $6) 60-piece puzzle that includes an alphabet trail. (800) 922-1194.

Comparison Shopper— USA and World Maps Puzzles

USA puzzle maps in frames are the place to start. Small World's wooden version ($22) has good graphics of products, landmarks, capitals, and a vinyl sheet for arranging pieces out of the frame. 6 & up. (310) 645-9680. A 60-piece **Carmen Sandiego US** or **World Map Puzzle** (Great American Puzzle Factory $11.95) has state names, some landmarks, and magic-rub clues for solving crime cases. 6 & up. (800) 922-1194. Testers liked the huge **World Map** (Frank Schaffer $13.95) 100-piece 20" x 30" puzzle. Names of the continents and oceans are printed on map and includes 21 geography cards to match icons on the map. Says 5 & up, we'd say 7 & up. (800) 421-5565. For more advanced puzzlers, try **USA Attractions** (Ravensburger $9.95), a 200-piece pictorial puzzle of USA. 9 & up. (800) 445-8347.

More Advanced Puzzles—100 Pieces + and Brainteasers

■ **Statue of Liberty Puzzle** ★ PLATINUM AWARD
(Frank Schaffer $14.95) You'll be impressed with the gigantic 20" x 44" tall illustration of Lady Liberty that grows out of this 100 piece giant floor puzzle. Not simple, since the colors and folds look very much the same. Bring her out as a family project! 6 & up. (800) 421-5565.

■ **Connections** ★
(Tiger $29.99) Like your old Connect 4 strategy game,

the object here is to light up four disks in a row before your opponent does. This electronic version can be played against the machine or with another player. There are two games, one trickier than the other, and happily, it has a sounds-off button so you won't be hollering, "Stop!" Takes 4 AA batteries. 8 & up. Also top-rated from Tiger, **Brain Warp** (5 & up). (847) 913-8100.

■ **Stormy Seas** 🏆

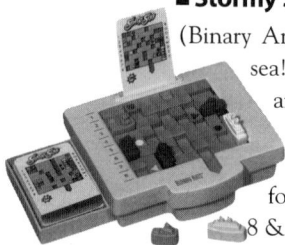

(Binary Arts $15) Picture your ship on the shifting sea! Use one of 40 cards to place ships and find an open channel to steer your boat to safety. This is a variation of **Rush Hour,** Platinum Award '98. Both are first-class brain teasers for developing visual perception and strategy. 8 & up. (703) 924-0243.

It's Magic!

Some kids like to impress friends and family with magic tricks. Learning to do them takes time, practice, and real reading skills. Reluctant readers may become avid readers of books that involve doing things such as magic or science experiments that are like magic. Our top picks for beginners are T.C. Timber's small kits, **Magic Disks** *and* **Abracadabra** *($9.95 each). 6 & up. (800) 245-7622. Also look at Milton Bradley's* **Magic Works** *($9 each). For a more elaborate set,* **Hocus Pocus** *(Small World $46) with dozens of tricks, props and a video. 8 & up. (310) 645-9680.*

Electronic Equipment & Learning Tools

Kids tend to love the novelty of electronic teaching machines, which don't actually teach new skills but do reinforce and provide the kind of practice some kids need.

■ **GeoSafari** and **GeoSafari Jr.** 🏆

(Educational Insights $99.95) We prefer the original **GeoSafari Jr.,** to the latest version featuring Richard Scarry's *Busytown.* While Scarry appeals to preschoolers, this product skills level (reading) is really for 6s & up. (They say 3 & up, we say more like 5 & up). **GeoSafari,** designed for 8 & up, includes pictorial quiz cards that focus on reading, math, weather, and history. The bells and whistles

makes head-to-head games more like playing Jeopardy. 8 & up. Platinum Award '94. (800) 933-3277.

Math & Magic ☞

(Chicco $27.99) Testers of mixed ages enjoyed this 4-level practice machine that works best with beginning addition/subtraction and computations that require regrouping (carrying) skills. Unlike many math machines, this takes answers the way kids learn to do them on paper, i.e., ones before the tens. 6–9. (877) 424-4226.

■ Multi Math ☞

(Play-Tech $19.99) This math quiz machine/calculator has two levels of difficulty, and drills addition, subtraction, multiplication, division, missing number/sign, and rounding up. Addition begins with double-digit numbers; answers are properly answered with ones before tens. Content is right for 6–10.

■ Twist & Shout Addition or Multiplication ☞

(Leap Frog $19.95 each) A flashlight-shaped, hand-held toy with 3 modes of play: One tells the answers; Two is a quiz with multiple choice answers; Three asks for missing factors. We wish it had a volume control. 6 & up. (800) 701-LEAP.

🛍 Comparison Shopper— Talking Globes ☞

GeoSafari Talking Globe Jr. ☞ PLATINUM AWARD

(Educational Insights $99.95) This "junior" version is much better suited to beginning geography skills than the original. This simpler globe is easy to read and use for finding answers to interactive questions. Pictorial/color cues help kids in guided explorations for 6–10s. The original **Geosafari Talking Globe** is still fine for 10s & up.(800) 933-3277. **The Odyssey Globe** (Explore Tech $299) is a much pricier interactive tool. Touch the sensor pen to this globe and it names the locale. In quiz mode, players must find a locale. Globe gives clues, and in search mode, you find

atlas info such as climate, population, and money, and even hear national anthems. 5–55+. (888) 456-2343.

■ Talking Whiz Kid Super Animated 🏆

(Vtech $59.99) We tested a slew of these "laptop" type quiz machines and this turned out to be the best fit for early school years. Many are just too hard for early school years and often the math answers need to be typed in with tens before ones—not the way kids do it on paper. This machine is on the mark and includes math (single- and two-column addition, subtraction, multiplication, and division), spelling, grammar, time, and music. It's easy to key in the activity of choice. 6–10. (800) 521-2010.

Phonics Toys

Phonics go in and out of style. The fact is, most kids learn to read with a mix of approaches, and these products provide playful practice:

■ Create-a-Word SuperMat

(Leap Frog $34.99) Put the giant (39" x 28") electronic Supermat on the floor or hang it on a wall and let the games begin! Kids push the letters printed on the talking mat and it says letters or sounds. Quiz mode asks child to find them. Younger kids use feet instead of hands. A three-letter word spelling game is for older players. A good toy for some 4s and up. For hands-on feedback with plastic letters that lift in and out, plus word cards that work on vowels, ends, and blends, **Leap Frog's Phonics Desk** ($49.95) is designed for beginning readers. For bilingual games, see **Phonics International English/Spanish** ($45). (800) 701-LEAP.

■ Phonics Fun

(Educational Insights $29.95) An electronic magic touch pen beeps as kids practice identifying initial sounds, blends, and vowels on 80 two-sided quiz cards. Better than most teaching machines, these are like an electronic "workbook" that also reinforces "reading" from left to right and from top to bottom. Says 4–8; we'd say better for 5s & up. (800) 933-3277.

Activity Kits and Art Supplies

For school-aged kids, art class is seldom long enough. Besides,

such classes are usually teacher-directed with little chance for kids to explore their own ideas.

Giving kids the tools and space for art projects at home is more than pure entertainment. Art helps develop their ability to communicate ideas and feelings visually, to refine eye/hand skills and learn how to stick with a task.

BASIC GEAR CHECKLIST FOR EARLY SCHOOL YEARS ARTISTS

✓ Crayons, chalk, colored pencils, and pastels
✓ Watercolor and acrylic paints
✓ Watercolor markers of varying thicknesses & colors
✓ Loom (weaving, beads, pot holders)

✓ Origami paper folding   ✓ Sand art supplies
✓ Sewing   ✓ Colored wax
✓ Lanyard kits   ✓ Needlepoint
✓ Rug hooking   ✓ Cutting/pasting
✓ Woodworking   ✓ Fabric paints
✓ Flower press   ✓ Air-hardening clay

Activity and Craft Kits

There are great choices this year in crafts that will appeal to both boys and girls, including making stickers, ceramic tiles, bouncing balls, and mobiles! School-aged kids love making something they can use or give as a gift. Some of our favorites introduce them to art forms and crafts from other cultures and times in history. Many will require adult assistance.

Painting, Coloring

■ Fuzzy Friends Treasure Boxes ⭐99⭐

(Crayola $8.99) A perfect craft kit for decorating three little treasure boxes to keep or give as gifts. Boxes in the shape of a cat, a fish and an elephant with lids are packed with pom-poms, eyes, markers, and a silver glitter pen. 5 & up. (800) CRAYOLA.

■ Hand Painted Ceramic Piggy Bank ☆ PLATINUM AWARD

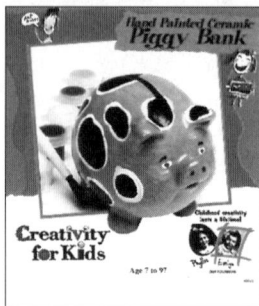

(Creativity for Kids $12) A chubby little white ceramic piggy bank comes ready to paint with spots, dots, hearts, or flowers—take your creative choices. Dry for 24 hours, then bake in a regular oven for a permanent finish. Adult supervision with baking. Our penny pinchers loved this one. 7 & up. Still top-rated, Platinum Award-winning **Hand Painted Ceramics Tiles** ($18) to design and bake, or a paint-and-bake **Ceramic Memory Plate** ☆ ($16). 8–98. (800) 642-2288.

■ Home Crafted Toys ☆

(Homecrafters $11) What could be better than three wooden toys in a kit? How about three wooden toys kids can make uniquely their own by painting them and even adding stickers for sizzle. This simple kit comes with a classic yo-yo a ball catcher and a wooden top. 5 & up. (770) 985-5460. For just a yo-yo, try Creativity for Kids' **Yo-Yo Kit** ☆ ($6) 7 & up. (800) 642-2288.

■ Illustory Kit

(Chimeric $19.95) Imagine the thrill of having an original story and your own illustrations bound in a real book. This kit comes with 12 sheets of paper with space for art on each and text (or you can opt for more text and less art). Mail your child's story in and get back a hard-covered book! What an inspiring way to motivate young writers. 5 & up. (800) 706-8697.

■ My Art Gallery ☆ PLATINUM AWARD

(Alex $30) Here are the ingredients for creativity—watercolors, oil pastels, markers, colored pencils, crayons, chalk, scissors, glue, big cardboard frames, and a box that turns into a portfolio for keeping young artists' creations. 5 & up. (800) 666-2539.

■ Paint the Wild Kits ☆

(Balitono $14 & up) Beautifully crafted wood carvings that kids can paint and display or use as play figures. New for ☆, sets of dinos, African animals, or horses. Also charming, a **Birdhouse Chime Kit** ($17) with a tiny songbird sitting on a miniature birdhouse with pre-

assembled wind chimes. For more advanced builders, choose a **Butterfly & Ladybug Wind Chime Kit** ($15) that kids assemble. Also, for holiday presents, our testers loved the **Christmas Ornaments** ($15) and an unusual **Nutcracker** ($17). 6 & up. (800) 769-9491.

■ **Under Sea Bag Buddies**

(Creativity for Kids $16) Move over, Beanie Babies—make way for these sand-filled creatures: a dolphin, a whale, and an octopus that kids paint with bright acrylic fabric paint. Once dry, these are fun to juggle, catch, or display. Science facts about creatures come with juggling tips. 6 & up. (800) 642-2288.

■ **Wooden Treasure Box**

(Creativity for Kids $16) Just right for holding special pins, rings, coins and treasures, this sturdy wooden box with a brass latch is ready to decorate with acrylic paints and brush for making it like no other box in the world. 7 & up. (800) 642-2288.

NOTABLE PREVIOUS WINNERS

Icky Sticky Bugs (Alex $10 each) Kids draw with colored glue onto a vinyl sheet. After drying, they lift off and stick to windows. 6 & up. (800) 666-2539. **Paint A Snake** and **Paint-A-Tyra-Dino** (Snakes & Things $7 & $16), small flexible wooden figures, wiggle when held and come with paints, brush, and glow-in-the-dark glaze. A quick, satisfying craft project. 5 & up. (800) 966-3762. **Shrinky Dink Art** (Mrs. B's $10 & up) Trace a design or create your own on vinyl sheets that are then cut and placed in the oven by an adult and magically they shrink! 6 & up. (800) 76-BEADS. **Tie Dye Wear Kit** (Jacquard $19.95) Comes with enough dyes and ideas for 16 tee shirts (not included). No heat needed. Adult supervision needed. (800) 442-0455.

Cut & Paste (and Glue!)

■ **Collage-a-Family**

(Alex $17) Tracing is not one of our things, but this kit involves a lot more. There's a family of cardboard dolls, patterns to cut out, and paper, plus glitter, buttons, doo-dads, etc., to dress the family. Glue them to colored wooden sticks and make up original stories. Combines art, dexterity, and language all in one package. 5 & up. (800) 666-2539.

■ **Gold Leaf Frame Kit** 🏅

(Creative Education of Canada $20) We were very impressed with the results of this special kit. Comes with wood frame, structural compound for adding designs, and glue that adheres the gold leaf to the frame. The gold leaf is very delicate to work with and is therefore intended for older kids and adults. (800) 982-2642.

■ **Flower Crazy Desk Set** 🏅 PLATINUM AWARD

(Learning Curve $16.99) A craft project for making a beautiful gift. Kit includes fixings for decorating a pencil holder and a note-pad with felt, glitter glue, jewels, and ric rac. A good introduction to decorating with felt—that may inspire other non kit-related creations. 5 & up. Also top-rated: **FeltKids Design Kits** 🏅 ($16.99), precut figures and clothes for kids who love to glue, glue, glue! Choose from mermaids, fairies, or glittering gowns. (800) 704-8697.

■ **Forever Together** 🏅

(Alex $13) There's nothing like getting organized so you can find your friends' phone numbers and keep track of birthdays and special memories. This well-made address book has firm covers to decorate and tie together with pages to fill with birthdates, favorite expressions, and other important facts. 7 & up. (800) 666-2539.

■ **Create Your Own Scrapbook** 🏅

(Creativity for Kids $20) Kids are great collectors, and having a scrapbook is one way to get their collectibles organized. Kit includes a notebook, markers, stickers, paper, glue, color foam pieces, plastic sleeves, and ideas. 6 & up. (800) 642-2288.

NOTABLE PREVIOUS WINNERS:

Ballet Bag (Alex $17) A pre-made pink and lavender drawstring bag for slippers and leotard that ballerinas can personalize with pearls, ribbons, and glitter. 7 & up. (800) 666-2539. **Legendary Worry Dolls** (Curiosity Kits $12.50) Based on folklore from the Andes, kids create their own worry dolls to tell their troubles to. Says 6 & up; we'd say more like 9 & up. (800) 584-KITS.

Candlemaking Kits

■ Beeswax Candles 🌟99

(Creativity for Kids $15) Everything needed to roll simple candles around a wick. 5 & up. (800) 642-2288. For 8s & up, Candlemaking Activity Kit (Curiosity Kits $8) comes with decorative sticks that demand more dexterity. No heat required for either kit. (800) 584-KITS.

Modeling & Molding

■ National Geographic Aborigine Pottery 🌟99

(Curiosity Kits $6.50) Air-hardening red clay can be shaped into pinch or coiled pots or slabs that are painted with symbols from ancient cultures. Clay has a distinctive odor that fades when it dries. 8 & up. (800) 584-KITS.

■ Wax Works

(Chenille Craft $4.95 & up) These waxy sticks (available in a rainbow of colors) can be coiled, twisted, and shaped into letters, butterflies, or free-form sculptures. Also, top-rated, **Creativity Street** ($14.95), a kit that includes Wax Works, pipe cleaners, eyes, feathers, and beads for creative fun. (800) 621-1261. 5 & up.

■ Copy Cast BLUE CHIP

(Creativity for Kids $16) An unusual casting kit that actually makes a reusable mold so that a cast of a hand, foot, or toy can be made again and again. Our testers insisted on cloning their action figures. (800) 642-2288.

NOT-TO-BE-MISSED PREVIOUS WINNERS

Chalk Factory (Alex $10) make your own chalk kit. 5 & up. (800) 666-2539. **Make-a-Mask Kit** (Educational Insights $12.95) Make original masks to wear or display. Comes with plastic reusable face form, plaster gauze, paint, and excellent step-by-step guide. (800)

933-3277. **Pottery Wheel** (Butterfly Company $30) gives kids a chance to try their hand at throwing a pot. Has a foot pedal and comes with two pounds of clay, tools, glaze. 8 & up. (516) 678-1700.

Jewelry & Accessory Kits

Stringing beads is more than a creative craft, it helps kids develop fine motor skills. A big kit is fun for a party or sleepover project.

■ Bead Bonanza

(Alex $20) Hundreds of metallic, jewel tone, letter, heart, and odd-shaped beads in a plastic box with compartments for each color. 5 & up. (800) 666-2539.

■ Leather Bracelets 🏅

(Creativity for Kids $10) Kids who may not be up to weaving friendship bracelets will have no trouble with these three leather ones that snap on and can be decorated in a snap with markers. A quick, easy, and pleasing project. (800) 642-2288.

■ National Geographic: World Jewelry

(Curiosity Kits $20) All the raw materials (including semi-precious stones) for creating beautiful African, Chinese, Peruvian, Venetian, and Egyptian jewelry with background about each culture. Or for more hands-on experience, bake your own with **Clay Bead Kit** ($12). 9 & up. (800) 584-KITS.

Sewing Kits

This category has exploded with great choices. Here are our testers' favorites:

■ Betty's Begin to Sew Sets 🏅

(Quincrafts $4.99 & up) Small affordable kits for trying out a variety of needle crafts. New for 🏅 : **Dolphin** or **Butterfly /Flower** bean bag sets come with plastic safety needle and pre-cut holes for easy sewing. 5 & up. Testers also liked the **Needlepoint Activity Deluxe Kit** ($7.99) with materials for using quickpoint to make picture frames, bookmark, earring stand, and keychain. A good place to start—fast and satisfying. 7 & up. (800) 342-8458.

■ **Dress Up Bears** ⭐99

(Alex $17 each) Last year's **Dress Up Bear** (in overalls) is joined by **Miss Dress Up Bear** with straw hat, precut fabric for a dress. Young sewers follow directions to assemble, sew, and embellish an outfit for their 10" bear. One tester says adult help will be needed for beginners. 7 & up. Platinum '98. Still recommended: **Sew Fun Dress Up Dolls** (Alex $20) Three 7" multicultural felt dolls with precut outfits to sew. 8 & up. Platinum Award '97. (800) 666-2539.

■ **National Geographic: Mola Pillow** ⭐99 **PLATINUM AWARD**

(Curiosity Kits $12) Fashioned like the multicolored layered cloth pictures from Panama, this kit makes a handsome pillow with precut felt. We loved it until we tried to stitch through the glued animal form. Don't do it! New directions will indicate that you sew around the animal—not through it. This makes a handsome project—too bad the directions got messed up. 8 & up. (800) 584-KITS.

■ **Sweet Dreams Pillow** ⭐99

(Learning Curve $16.99 each) Beginners loved these pre-cut felt sewing kits with the raw materials for making either a decorative pillow or 3 bean bag **Tropical Birdies** (or **Kitties**). Bean bag cushions are provided for stuffing—so no spilled beans (we couldn't resist). Comes with pins for basting and needles sharp enough for felt (unlike some other kits we tried this year)—but this also means that projects will need supervision. 7 & up. (800) 704-8697.

■ **National Geographic: My World Quilt**

(Curiosity Kits $20) Kids create their own quilt by drawing pictures onto preprinted panels with headings such as, "This is my family," "This is my town," "...my street," then ironing the panels and sewing them together. 7 & up with adult assistance. Platinum Award '97. (800) 584-KITS.

🛍️ Comparison Shopper— Weaving Looms

Begin to Weave (Quincrafts $4.99) has a cardboard "loom," a blunt needle, yarn, and some beads for extra finishing touches. A simple way to introduce weaving to beginners. (800) 342-8458. **PegLoom** (Harrisville Designs $18.95) a small over/under loom with large needle is also a good choice for true beginners. 5 & up. **Create Your Own Loops & Loom Projects** (Woodkrafters $14) potholder looms are fine for beginners. This new 7" x 7" frame comes with fabric loops and a metal hook that's easier to use than most kits that come with plastic. 5 & up. (800) 345-3555.

For larger looms: Brio's **Loom** ($65) comes out of the box threaded and ready to work! Testers felt the instructions were spotty for a true novice but gave the product overall high ratings for design. (888) 274-6869. The Harrisville **Easy Weaver** ($90) also comes threaded but does not fold up like Brio's. Our testers found the instructions easier to follow and also liked the refill kits ($25.95) that slip right onto the loom! 7 & up. Harrisville's new **Needlepoint Kit** ($12.95) comes with scrumptious colors and plastic frames. (800) 338-9415.

Art with a Scientific Edge

■ All About Paper Making 🎖️99

(DaMert $16) Use your blender and junk mail to make recycled paper. Kit comes with clear directions, simple tools, and dried flowers for making scented paper, too. Also, **Sun Print Making Kit,** with all the ingredients for making designs with light-sensitive paper. 8 & up. (800) 231-3722.

■ Color Catchers! 🎖️99

(Koosh Creative/Odds On $10) Kids peel and stick vinyl shapes onto the plastic sheets that look like "stained glass" panels. By layering yellow on blue or magenta they "mix" colors. Once the panel is complete it lifts and sticks to a wall or window. Develops kids dexterity as well as ability to follow directions and stick to a task with relatively quick results. 6 & up. (800) 755-6674.

■ Glow In the Dark 3-D City & Lunar Activity Kit 🌟

(Great Explorations $12.50 & $15 each) The coolest way to learn how phosphorescent pigments absorb and give off light is to play with either of these sets. Testers made 3-D sculptures with star-and-moon-shaped plastic disks of the 3-D Star City. They loved decorating forms with stencils, special paints, glitter, and glow-in-the-dark stickers that add a luminous glow to bikes, rooms, and notebooks. This company's **Glow-in-the-Dark Ball & Jax** set is also really fun. 5 & up. (800) 347-4818.

■ Crank It! Kits

(Woodkrafter $20 each) Our testers were thrilled with the results of building these witty wooden 6"–10" moving sculptures. We still love the **Happy Clapper** as an end-of-year gift to applaud a teacher, the **Wave,** and the **Caterpillar.** All help kids discover how simple machines work. Unfortunately, the directions in the new dinosaurs and scorpion kits were not clear. Adult help needed for younger builders. 10 & up. Platinum '98. (800) 345-3555.

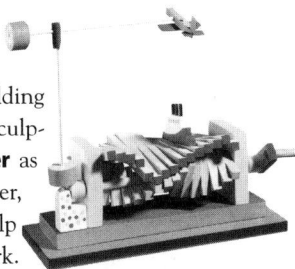

■ Leaf Press Activity Kit 🌟

(Alex $18) We liked the fact that this kit also came with the material for making a journal for a leaf collection. 7 & up. (800) 666-ALEX.

■ Lego Crazy Action Contraptions 🌟

(Klutz $19.95) Lots of small action Lego projects that won't take a year and a day to build. Comes with a supply of Lego Technic pieces for building five contraptions and plans for five more with the addition of standard Lego pieces that almost every kid already owns. We like the M&M dispenser—too bad no M&Ms are included. 7 & up.

■ Makit & Bakit Sets 🌟

(Quincrafts $10) You probably made these when you were a kid. Pour colorful crystals into a grid, bake them in the oven. Use as keychains or suncatchers. We liked the glow in the dark set with less gender-specific themes. Adult supervision. 8 & up. (800) 704-8697.

■ Super Dooper Bouncing Zooom Balls 🌟

(Curiosity Kits $10) An update of a '98 Platinum award winner, this kit has enough material for 10 balls with new shapes—a 10-sided ball, a bumpy one, a scalloped one plus the original round jax-sized ball. A little science here with mixing crystals & water to change them into a solid, bounceable material in just 3 minutes. 6 & up. (800) 584-KITS.

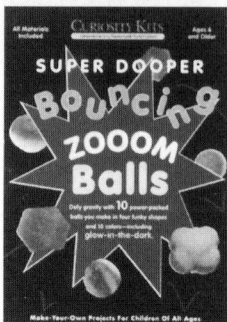

NOT-TO-BE-MISSED PREVIOUS WINNERS

Marbling (Creativity for Kids $18) Oil and water don't mix and that's the secret magic of this age-old art form. Kit includes nontoxic ink, a pan, templates for boxes, paper, and materials for making a book cover and other marbled objects. Use rubber gloves and a bigger pan than the one provided in kit. 8 & up. Platinum Award '96. (800) 642-2288. Also top-rated, **Beeswax Candles** (Creativity for Kids $15) Everything needed to roll simple candles around a wick. No heat required—so kids can easily do this project. 5 & up. (800) 642-2288. Also, **Candle-making Activity Kit** (Curiosity Kits $8) Wax sheets and decorative sticks that demand more dexterity. 8 & up. (800) 584-KITS.

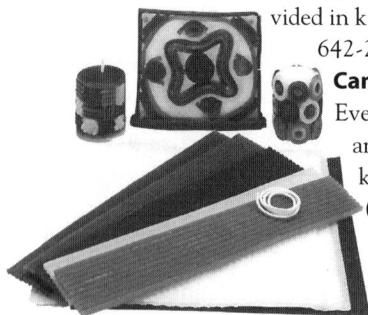

Stamp-A-Mania

■ Pooh Letters & Numbers 🌟

(All Night Media $15) Older fans of Pooh will enjoy stamping out words with this 36-piece collection that includes the alphabet and numbers decorated with Pooh and his friends. Also top-rated, **Polar Animals** ($10) includes a seal, polar bear, walrus, wolf, fox, penguin, and whale. (800) 782-6733.

■ Stamp-a-Face

(All Night Media $15) Zany eyes, mouths, noses, hairdos, ears, and claws combine for making cartoons or cards. Develops creative thinking, dexterity, and attention to details. Also useful, a set of **Alphabeasts & Numbirds** ($15): letters and numbers with animals for signs, cards, and captions. Long-time favorites, **Stamp-A-Story Adventures** ($20 each set) are ideal for illustrating child-made storybooks. Testers loved fairy tale & neighborhood adventure themes. (800) 782-6733.

Musical Instruments

■ Chimalong and Mini Chimalong ⭐⁹⁹

(Woodstock Percussion $20 & up) Unlike most musical toys for kids, the tone of this metal-chime xylophone is lovely. Can be played by number/color or musical notation. Can be enjoyed by a preschooler, but becomes a true musical instrument for older children that also reinforces reading from left to right. New mini version is not as sweet and the tiny chimes are harder to hit with precision. That said, this is a pleasant travel take-along toy with color- and number-coded music and well-designed "easel" that holds the instrument as well as music. Says 3 & up; we'd say 4–8. (914) 331-7728.

■ Glockenspiel Making Kit ⭐⁹⁹

(Woodstock Percussion $15) As usual, this maker has designed a musical toy with beautiful sound quality as well as an innovative design. Children "construct" the playing pieces of this instrument by placing them on the frame in size and number order. Chimes attach easily with Velcro. Putting the playing pieces on, kids see and feel the progressive size and discover which keys are higher and lower. A wonderful tool for musical exploration. Kids can play tunes with number or notation. Says 4 & up, but 5–8s will get more play and learning from this kit. Also top-rated: **Rainstick Kit** ($20) and **Mbira Kit** ($20).. (914) 331-7728.

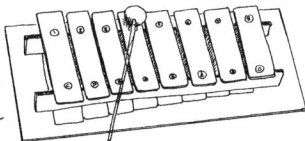

■ Kids' Tom Tom ⭐⁹⁹

(Remo/Woodstock Percussion $38) If you're lucky, they'll let you play this colorful drum while they dance—or switch roles and boogie! Comes with mallets, but testers say that tones are better when played by hand. Also terrific: a **Kids' Konga Drum, Two-Headed Bongo,** and **Ocean Drum.** New for '99, a **Kids' Djembe** ($38). (914) 331-7728.

■ Music Maker Harp BLUE CHIP

(Peeleman-McLaughlin $50) No electronic
sounds here. This is a cross between a
zither and an autoharp, but much easier
to learn to play. Slip one of 12 follow-
the-dot song sheets under the strings and
pluck. Has a soft and lovely tone. Includes folk,
Beatles, and classical music sheets. 6 & up. (800) 779-2205.

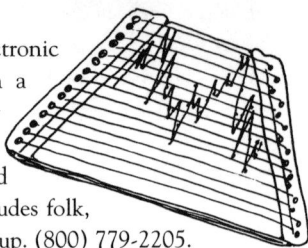

■ Piano Keyboard

(Casio $40–$150) Without a huge investment, an electronic keyboard gives kids a
taste of what learning to play the piano is
like. Keyboards from 32 to 49 keys are
for young kids. For 8s & up consider four-
to five-octave keyboards ($149 & up). O.K.,
it's not a Steinway, but for tight space and budget it's a
place to start. 6 & up. For a less complex keyboard, **Little Smart
Super Sound Works** (VTech $39.95) A 24-note keyboard with
songs, instruments, animal sounds, color-coded music, and follow-
the-light mechanism. 4–7. (800) 521-2010.

Active Play

*Young school kids are often more eager than able to play many
games with rules. Sometimes the real equipment is too heavy for
them to use. Balls that are softer don't hurt as much and promote
kids' confidence. The same is true of scaled-down bats, rackets,
and other equipment.*

Ball Games Equipment

■ Gripper Balls

(Saturnian 1 $17.99) Designed for beginners, these balls are covered
with nylon in bright neon colors with non-slip grips. There's a lightweight bat and ball, a terrific football, soccer ball, volley ball plus a
small mitt with grippers and ball for young catchers. 5 & up. (800)
653-2719. Also: **BLUE CHIP Nerf Balls** (Hasbro $7 & up)
are also lighter than the real thing and safer for
beginners. (800) 327-8264.

■ Koosh Catchers

(OddzOn $19.99) Even the poorest catchers

will have success with these bristled disks that attach with adjustable velcro straps and easily grab the looped Koosh ball. Good for learning to keep your eye on the ball. 7 & up. (800) 755-6674.

■ Thumb Ball 🌟

(Saturnian 1 $16.99) An all-new way to play catch! Players press a thumb over the thumb activated-suction cup handle to capture the big 9" ball. Toss the ball and lift a thumb— the vacuum is broken and ball is released. Takes practice, but it's an innovative way to play catch. 7 & up. (800) 653-2719.

Shopping Tip— Basketball Sets

Several companies make adjustable basketball hoops for young players. Some with cardboard posts and electronic scorekeepers are fun but for indoor use only. Best choices are from Little Tikes, Fisher-Price, and Ohio Arts. For older players, go to a sporting goods store for a real backboard.

■ Turbo Hoops 🌟

(Hedstrom $80) Forget the arcade—now they can play hoops at home! Scaled for kids, this hoops game has an electronic scorer, comes with three balls, and folds against the wall when not in use. Takes patience to assemble and 4 AA batteries. New for 🌟, a taller version was not available for testing. 5 & up. Platinum Award '98. (800) 233-3271.

At the Beach

■ Beachbowl

(Do things $14) Press the numbered cups into the sand, put the backer board in place, and get ready to bowl! A fun game for mixed ages when kids need something to do out of the water. 4 & up. (888) 726-3869.

■ Beachworks

(Eagle $20) For serious castle builders, the 11-piece tool set and waterproof booklet will guide all members of the family in building the castle of their dreams. With forms for making stairs, watchtowers, battlements, and towers, this is an open-ended kit for beach buddies of all ages. 6 & up. (800) 643-6798.

Wheel Toys

🛍 Shopping Checklist

⊗ Fives will continue to enjoy many of the wheel toys in the Preschool section.

⊗ By six or seven, most kids are ready and eager for a two-wheeler with training wheels. Steer clear of bikes with gears or hand brakes. Learning to balance is a big enough deal.

⊗ Tempting as it may be to surprise your child, your best bet is to take your child to the store.

⊗ Buy a bike that fits, rather than one to "grow into." When kids straddle a bike they should be able to put a foot on the ground for balance.

⊗ Budget and size will dictate the choices. Schwinn ($100 & up) and Huffy ($100 & up) offer solidly built 16" bikes with adjustable training wheels and an assortment of accessories.

⊛ Helmets do help! According to the Consumer Product Safety Commission, one in seven children suffers head injuries in bike-related accidents. While studies show that wearing helmets reduces the risk of injury by 85 percent, the sad fact is that only 5 percent of bike-riding kids actually wear helmets. See Safety Guidelines for new helmet standards.

Science Toys and Equipment

Science is still best understood with hands-on materials. Favorite equipment: magnifiers, magnets, gyroscopes, kaleidoscopes, prism,s and a compass.

■ **Activity Rock Kit** 🎯

(GeoCentral $18.95) If you have a budding rock collector in your family, this kit is a sure fire hit. Comes with activity book and 12 minerals that have special attributes sure to wow friends and family. For example, there's optical calcite, floating pumice, and magnetic lodestone. Specialty stores.

🛍️ **Comparison Shopper— Archeological Dig Kits** 🎯

We thought this kind of kit was pretty mindless, but our testers loved playing archeologist, chipping away at a clay block to unearth hidden treasures. For younger diggers, we found **Buried Treasure Kits** (Educational Insights $17.95 each) Choose from **Castle, Egyptian,** or **Maya Treasure Kit.** Facts about the period they are digging into are included with age-appropriate tools. 7 & up. (800) 933-3277. **National Geographic Expedition Series** (Kristal $20 each), which includes a splendid **Chinese Terra-Cotta Figure** or a **Dinosaur Egg,** have more fine details for older kids and looked exceptional, but final product was not ready for testing. (206) 720-6264.

Birdhouses & Feeders

There are more bird kits around than ever. Many did not test well. The easiest of the precut, glue-together models are by Woodkrafters ($12 & up). A feeder with plastic side windows needs only wood glue to put together. The nail-together models did not test well. 6 & up. (800) 345-3555. For fancier precut houses, consider **Colonial Bird Houses** ($12 & up). (508) 838-2601.

■ **Butterfly Garden & Ladybug Lodge**

(Insect Lore $21.95) These kits match kids' fascination with bugs—

front-row seats to the metamorphosis of a caterpillar. Have kids keep a journal of the wonderful transformation from caterpillar to Painted Lady butterfly. Comes with butterfly box, instructions on their care, and a certificate to mail in for 3–5 butterflies. Also fascinating, a **Ladybug Lodge** ($14.95) with a log and experiments to study the 75 ladybugs that you send for, keep for a week, and release to feast on your garden's aphids. (800) LIVE-BUG.

Comparison Shopper—Gear Sets

A great solo toy that develops math, motor, and thinking skills as kids make moving "machines." **Gears! Gears! Gears!** (Learning Resources $20 & up) has a variety of gear toys that are easier to manipulate for younger kids. We like their 95-piece set with one size gear ($19.95) or the huge 150-piece Super Set in a bucket ($40). New and truly wonderful for ⚞, **Gears! Gears! Gears! Gizmos** ($29.95) is a far more complex 82-piece set with small, medium, and large gears and bases, plus spring connectors, spiral patterned gears, and propeller for special effects! If you already own Gears! add a **Whirligig, Roundabout,** or **Pulley Accessory set** ($10 each). For a scientific edge, **Gears & Pulleys** ($20), has fewer gears but is an excellent activities kit developed at Chicago's Museum of Science. 6 & up. (800) 222-3909. Older kids love **Kaleidocolor** (International Playthings $27), a 48-piece set of multi-sized gears with optical patterns. Greater dexterity needed to fit these into base plates. They say 3–8; we say 5–8+. (973) 831-1400.

Magnets

Marvelous Magnets (Alex $20) *A hands-on kit filled with projects and experiments includes ten different types of magnets. 7 & up.* (800) 666-2539. **Magnetic Explorer** (*Educational Insights*

$14.95) does not have as many projects, but all of the magnets are stored in a fold-up container that fits on a belt loop. (800) 933-3277.

■ **Nature Station** 🏅

(HSP $20) A mini ecosystem that comes with everything needed for hands-on experiments. Kit has soil, seeds, trays, pyramid-shaped covers, plus a 40-page booklet with ideas for testing water, soil, sprouting seeds, and keeping records. 8 & up. Still top-rated, **Root-vue.** (619) 423-9399.

New Ways of Looking— Observation Tools

■ **Construct a Scope**

(Learning Resources $38) Our 10-year-old tester started using this science kit by following projects in the book but before long was combining lenses to make inventions of his own. He gave this high ratings but because there are so many parts in the kit he suggested numbering them to match the diagram. 9 & up. (800) 222-3909.

■ **Perfect Shot 35mm Camera**

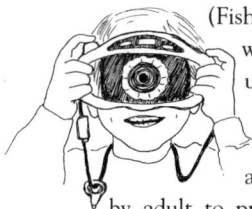

(Fisher-Price $24.99) Better than its predecessor which used 110 film with grainy results, this uses 35 mm film and produces good photos. Dual-eye viewfinder is a plus, so kids don't have to close one eye. Built-in flash with automatic shut-off and film loading is done by adult to prevent accidental film exposure. 5 & up. Platinum Award '98. (800) 432-5437.

■ **Giant Periscope**

(Tasco $15) For exploring around corners, this sturdy plastic double-handled periscope is just right. This company also makes a full line of microscopes and telescopes. (305) 591-3670.

■ **Odyssey Scope**

(Rainbow Products $15) Here's a kaleidoscope that looks like a microscope. It has a rotating disc and comes with 50 holographic magnetic shapes that stick to the disc and can be arranged and rearranged in ever-changing patterns. Platinum Award '96. 7 & up. (541) 826-9007.

Telescopes and Microscopes

>  **Comparison Shopper—Microscopes 50x**
> Testers report that both Uncle Milton's **Super GeoScope** ($33.50) and Educational Insights' **Deluxe Magniscope** ($34.95) vie feature-for-feature for best scope. Though optics were a bit better in the GeoScope, testers liked Magniscope's tilting base and multiple ways of holding specimens. Removed from the stand for field use, testers found the built-in spacer on the GeoScope made it easier to focus. Both companies offer hand-held 30x models, of which our testers gave higher marks to GeoScope, because it's easier to focus. 6 & up. Uncle Milton (818) 707-0800 / Educational Insights (800) 933-3277.

■ Galactic Explorer

(Educational Insights $39.95) This is not a high-powered telescope, but unlike all too many kids' scopes, this one works pretty well. It has interchangeable 50x and 100x eyepieces, comes on a full-sized adjustable tripod, and includes a wide-field 3x finder scope and a guide with tips on viewing the moon. 8 & up. (800) 933-3277.

■ I Made My Microscope
& I Made My Telescope

(Homecrafter $13 each) Our testers have consistently loved this series of hands-on science kits. **I Made My Telescope** (in ten easy steps, really!); **I Made My Kaleidoscope** with unbreakable Mylar mirrors and an end piece that can be loaded with ever-changing contents. A great parent/child project for 5s–7s or solo for 8 & up. Also top-rated, **I Made My Periscope** ($15). (770) 985-5460.

Best Travel Toys and Games

As kids get older they enjoy traditional games such as **I Spy, Twenty Questions, Geography,** or **Facts of Five.** They are also ready for word games and travel books. Be sure to bring along some story tapes (see Audio Chapter). Aside from classics such as **Slide Puzzles** (DaMert), **Scrabble**

(Milton Bradley), and **Etch-a-Sketch** *(Ohio Arts), here are some other neat take-alongs:*

■ Are We There Yet ? 🏅

(Are We There Yet? $14.95) Warning! The driver may not play! Other than that, this is a game for good fun while keeping travelers on the lookout for such things as 3 people in the back seat of a car, an uprooted tree, a white house with blue trim. Winner is the one with most cards. 7 & up. (800) 892-9012.

■ Feltkids Interactive Playbooks 🏅

(Learning Curve $24.99 each) Our favorites this year: **Decorate and Play House, Discovering Animal Habitat,** & **Let's Put On a Show** provide for expanding language, original storytelling, and good parent/child connections. They say 3 & up, we think 5s would also enjoy this product independently. (800) 704-TOYS.

■ Lego Backpack Set 🏅

(Lego $25) For on-the-go-builders, this sturdy backpack comes with 486 Lego Freestyle bricks and room to spare for packing other take-alongs. 5–10. (800) 233-8756.

■ Magnetic Chess 🏅

(Educational Insights $9.95) The pieces on this folding magnetic set are a reasonable size (not the usual itsy-bitsy) and store in the fold-up board. Magnetic checkers also available. 8 & up. (800) 933-3277.

■ Tic Tac Twice Insects or Animals 🏅

(Aristoplay $10 each) Tuck this nifty little game for two into a bag for a way to make time fly. Take turns covering matching pictures on both playing boards with magnetic discs—the winner is first to cover four in a row. 6 & up. (888) GR8-GAME.

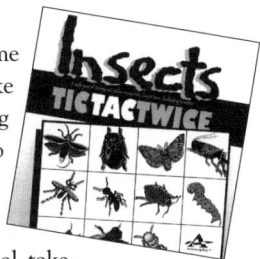

■ Mini-Chimalong 🏅

(Woodstock Percussion $20) A pleasant travel take-along toy with color- and number-coded music and well-designed "easel" that holds the instrument as well as music. It all slips into a plastic carrying bag. Says 3 & up; we'd say 4–8. (800) 435-8863.

■ Poseable Madeline

(Eden $16) Unlike fashion dolls, this 8" storybook doll is a girl with easy-to-handle clothes and accessories like a camping set, scout's outfit, and travel case. (800) 443-4275.

■ **Port to Port Puzzle**

(Binary Arts $10) Shift the tiles up, down, and sideways to get the three pieces of your ship in order and from one port to another. A challenging brainteaser. 8 & up. (703) 924-0243.

■ **Radio Watch** ➤99¢

(Wild Planet $14) A very cool watch with small earphones that pick up both AM and FM stations. We were impressed with the sound quality of the radio. A great gift that both Mom and Dad will want to borrow. (800) 247-6570.

■ **Wonderboards**

(Dowling $12) Ideal for travel, these 9" x 12" magnetic boards come with flexible magnetic "puzzle" pieces with themes such as build-a-bug, make-a-snake, or create-a-castle that will keep kids on the go busy. 5 & up. (800) MAGNET-1.

Best Birthday Gifts for Every Budget

Big Ticket $100 plus	**Rokenbok Expandable RC Building System** (Rokenbok), **Odyssey Globe** (Explore Tech), or **Chaos** (Chaos)
Under $100	**GeoSafari Talking Globe Jr.** (Educational Insights), or **American Girls Collection Doll** (Pleasant Co.), or **Turbo Hoops** (Hedstrom)
Under $75	**Celestial Stinger** (Lego Systems), or **Music Maker Harp** (Peeleman-McLaughlin), or **Global Friends Doll** (Global Friends)
Under $50	**Create-a-Word Supermat** (Leapfrog), or **Solar Powered Kínex Stunt Kit** (K'nex)
Under $40	**Tyco Revolver R/C Stunt Vehicle** (Mattel), or **Muffy VanderBear with Tea Set** (North American Bear), or **Finger Puppet Theater** (Manhattan Toy)

Under $30	**Medieval Castle Theater** (Creative Ed. Of Canada), or **Les Mini Corolline** (Corolle)
Under $25	**Round the Bend** (International Playthings), or **X-V Racers Cyclone** (Mattel), or **MiniChimalong** (Woodstock Percussion)
Under $20	**Birdhouse Chime Kit** (Balitono), or **Flower Crazy Desk Set** (Learning Curve), or **Rush Hour** (Binary Arts), or **Radio Watch** (Wild Planet)
Under $15	**Statue of Liberty Puzzle** (Frank Schaffer), or **Hand Painted Ceramic Piggy Bank Kit** (Creativity for Kids), or **Forever Together** (Alex)
Under $10	**Pivot** (Wizards of the Coast), or **Zooom Ball Kit** (Curiosity Kit), **Medieval Lacing Puppets** (Lauri), or **Leather Bracelets Kit** (Creativity for Kids), or **Glow-in-the-Dark Ball & Jax** (Great Exploration)

Using Ordinary Toys for Kids with Special Needs

This is a sampling of new Special Needs Adaptable Product (SNAP) Awards for 1999. Many toys throughout this book will be of interest to kids with special needs. For a full chapter of SNAP award winners, see our companion book, **Oppenheim Toy Portfolio 1999 Edition: The Best Toys, Books, Videos, Music & Software For Kids,** *and visit our website, www.toyportfolio.com, throughout the year.*

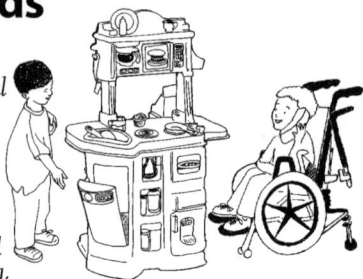

1999 SNAP Awards

■ Slumbertime Soother

(Fisher-Price $34.99) This crib toy has lights that change with the music or soothing nature sounds that provide added stimulation. An innovative remote control restarts music from 20 feet away so you don't need to go into the nursery to keep it going. (800) 435-5437.

■ Activity Table

(Fisher-Price $29.99) The best activity table we've seen in years, with a removable activity board that can be used on the floor. One side of the board has whirling marbles (safely enclosed); mirror; and flippers. The other side has a surface for stacking blocks with a chute for putting blocks away. **Activity Tip:** Play a game "bye-bye blocks" as you disappear the blocks down the chute. Another way for kids to learn that objects out of sight are not gone forever. (800) 432-5437.

■ Barney Song Magic Banjo

(Playskool $29.99) This stringless purple banjo has a hole where the strings would normally be. Put a hand in the hole to activate the music. It really is "magical" and will motivate kids to explore cause and effect as they use their hands to start and stop the music, even if a child cannot hold the instrument. (800) PLAYSKL.

■ Dunk & Clunk Circus Rings

(Sassy $8.50) Multi-textured rings and rattles slip into special slots in the lid of this see-through container. Beginners will like tasting, tossing and dropping pieces into the plastic box, but will eventually use this innovative sorter to develop wrist and finger action. (800) 323-6336.

■ Elmo & His Pet Puppy

(Tyco $29.99) New and novel, Elmo has controls in his hands that activate the radio-controlled puppy. For kids with difficulty gripping, try **Elmo's RC Stunt Plane.** (800) 488-8697.

■ Follow-the-Lights Talking Phone

(Mattel $30) Our testers enjoyed following the numbers and lights to dial Mickey and his friends. Phone can be programmed to teach child's home number. **Activity Tip:** Take turns repeating color and/or number sequences. (800) 524-8697.

■ Little Leap

(Leap Frog $39.99) This huggable frog plays games with letters and sounds, and it's polite, too. Unlike other quiz machines this does not limit answers to what comes before or after a letter or number to the one letter or number. It cues kids to see multiple answers. Kids with limited gripping power may have trouble activating Frog's hands. (800) 701-LEAP.

■ Puzzle Cube

(Wimmer-Ferguson $16) Testers loved playing "now you see it, now you don't" with this reversible fabric cube with openings for shapes. The textures and varying sounds of each shape provide sensory cues. Unlike most shape sorters, these shapes fit into any opening. (800) 747-2454.

■ Sort 'n Go Car

(Vtech $14.98) A jaunty yellow vehicle has musical shape-sorter windows that plays a different tune as each shape is placed inside the car. They all empty out of the trunk. We applaud the volume control on this toy. Can be used as a pull toy. (800) 521-2010.

■ Pippy Pals Dress Me Up Kids

(Pamela Drake $11.95) For kids who don't have the dexterity to sew, cut, or paste, this wooden doll frame has fabric choices that stay in place with a "frame" that closes over the edges of the doll. Pippy has four faces for changing moods. Available as boy or girl, and several ethnic variations. (800) 966-3762.

■ Threading Cheese & Apple

(Learning Curve $11.99 each) A wedge of cheese with a mouse on a string and a big red apple with a green worm are fun to lace in and out of holes. There's no right or wrong way, but either provides play-ful motivation for using those fine eye/hand skills. (800) 704-8697.

Safety Guidelines

Many people assume that before toys reach the marketplace they are subjected to the same kind of governmental scrutiny as food and drugs. The fact is that although the government sets specific safety standards, there is no agency like the FDA that pretests and approves or disapproves products.

The toy industry is charged with the responsibility to comply with federal safety standards, but they are self-regulating, which means it's not until there are complaints or reports of accidents that the Consumer Product Safety Commission (CPSC) enters into the picture. The CPSC is the federal government agency charged with policing the toy industry—but not until the products are already on the shelf!

What does all this mean to you as a consumer? Basically it means "Let the buyer beware!" Both small and large manufacturers have run into problems with small parts, lead paint, strangulation hazards and projectile parts.

The CPSC releases useful recall warnings that are posted in most major toy stores, and manufacturers are required to release recalls to the wire services. The CPSC has a hotline if you want further information about a recalled product or want to report one that perhaps should be recalled; you can call (800) 638-CPSC. The CPSC also publishes a safety handbook that you can request.

To protect your child, here is a safety checklist to keep in mind when you're shopping for playthings:

For infants and toddlers:

- **Dolls and stuffed animals.** Select velour, terry or non-fuzzy fabrics. Remove any and all bows, bells and doo-dads that can be swallowed. Stick to dolls with stitched-on features rather than buttons and plastic parts that may be bitten or pulled off.
- **Crib toys.** Toys should never be attached to an infant's crib with any kind of ribbon, string or elastic. Babies

and their clothing have been known to get entangled and strangled by such toys.

- **Soft but safe.** Be sure that soft toys such as rattles, squeakers and small dolls are not small enough to be compressed and possibly jammed into a baby's mouth.

- **Heirlooms.** Antique rattles and other treasures often do not meet today's safety standards and can be a choking hazard.

- **Wall hangings and mobiles.** Decorative hangings near or on the crib are interesting for newborns to gaze at but pose a safety hazard once a child can reach out and touch. They need to be removed when an infant is able to touch them.

- **Foam toys.** Avoid foam toys that can be chewed on and swallowed and present a choking hazard.

- **Push-and-straddle toys.** If you're looking for your child's first push toy, make sure it's stable and your child can touch the ground when sitting on the toy.

- **Toy chests.** Old toy chests with lids that can fall do not meet today's safety standards. They can severely injure and even entrap small children. New chests have removable lids or safety latches. We recommend open shelves and containers for safe and easy access instead of the jumble of a deep toy chest.

- **Age labels and small parts.** When you see a toy labeled "Not for children under 3," that's a warning signal! It usually means there are small parts. Such products are unsafe for toddlers—no matter how smart they may be! They are also unsafe for some threes and fours who frequently put things in their mouths.

- **Batteries.** Toys that run on batteries should be designed so that kids cannot get to the batteries.

- **Quality control.** Run your fingers around edges of toys to be sure there are no rough, sharp or splintery, hidden thorns. Check for products that can entrap or pinch little fingers.

For older children:

- **Eye and ear injuries.** Avoid toys with flying projectiles. Many action figures come with a number of small projectile parts that can pose a safety hazard if pointed in the wrong direction and that certainly pose a danger if there are younger children in the house.

- **High-power water guns.** Doctors report many emergency room visits from children with eye and ear abrasions caused by the trendy high-powered water guns.

- **Burns.** Avoid toys that heat up when used. Many of the toy ovens and baking toys become hot enough to cause burns.

- **Safety limits.** Establish clear rules with kids for sports equipment, wheel toys, and chemistry sets.

- **Adult supervision.** Avoid toys labeled "Adult supervision required" if you don't have the time or patience to be there.

For mixed ages:

Families with children of mixed ages need to establish and maintain safety rules about toys with small parts.

- Older children need a place where they can work on projects that younger sibs can't get hurt by or destroy.

- Establishing a work space for the older sib gives your big child the privilege of privacy along with a sense of responsibility.

- Old toys need to be checked from time to time for broken parts, sharp edges, or open seams. Occasionally clearing out the clutter can foster heightened interest in playtime. It also brings old gems to the surface that may have been forgotten.

New Safety Standard for Bike Helmets

We applaud the new federal safety standard that all bike helmets will need to meet by February 1999. Do little kids really need helmets? Look at the data and you decide:

About 900 people, including more than 200 children, are

killed annually in bicycle-related incidents; about 60% of these deaths involve a head injury. Data shows that very young bike riders incur a higher proportion of head injuries! More than 500,000 people are treated annually in U.S. emergency rooms for bicycle-related injuries. Research indicates that a helmet can reduce the risk of head injury by up to 85%!

New helmets must adequately protect the head, and have chin straps strong enough to prevent the helmet from coming off in a crash, collision, or fall. Helmets for children up to age five will cover more of the head to provide added protection to the more fragile areas of a young child's skull. New helmets will carry a label stating that they meet CPSC's new standards, to eliminate confusion about which certification mark to look for on helmets.

CPSC offers the following tips on how to wear a helmet correctly:

- Wear the helmet flat atop your head, not tilted back at an angle.

- Make sure the helmet fits snugly and does not obstruct your field of vision.

- Make sure the chin strap fits securely and that the buckle stays fastened.

Noisy Toys

In addition to all the above criteria, we have always considered the noise level of products. Loud toys are more than just annoying—they can actually pose a risk to your child's hearing. This year, with the generous assistance of Nancy Nadler of the League for the Hard of Hearing, we tested the sound level of many new toys. In doing so, we discovered that many ordinary rattles and squeakers produce sounds measured at 110 to 130 decibels. Yet experts say that sustained exposure, over time, to noise above 85 decibels will cause hearing damage. Because current regulations allow manufacturers to make toys which produce sounds up to 138 decibels at a distance of 25cm, parents must be informed consumers. We suggest that you:

- consider noise levels of toys before purchasing them.

- remember that musical toys, such as electric guitars, drums, and horns, emit sounds as loud as 120 decibels.

- stop and listen before purchasing a toy that makes a noise. If it sounds too loud for your ears, it probably is! Don't buy it.

- be very careful with toys designed to go next to the ear (such as toy phones and toys with headsets).

- remember that noisy floor toys are best listened to at a distance... teach your child not to place his ears on the speaker of the toy.

These guidelines have been prepared in conjunction with the League for the Hard of Hearing.

Subject Index

For the latest product reviews, updates, and recalls, subscribe to the Oppenheim Toy Portfolio Quarterly Newsletter.
The only independent guide to children's media.
Full year only $12

Name_____

Address _____

City/State/Zip _____

Send check to: Oppenheim Toy Portfolio, Inc., 40 East 9th Street, Suite 14M, New York, NY 10003, or call (212) 598-0502.

And visit our website at www.toyportfolio.com.